I0784068

That Was
Hugo Blythe MP

***Also by Peter Cowlam**

FICTION PRINT
Across the Rebel Network
Early Novels and Short Fiction
Marisa
New King Palmers†
Who's Afraid of the Booker Prize?††
Utopia

FICTION EBOOK
A Forgotten Poet
Call Bridgland Jolley
Marisa
The Concord Diary

FICTION AUDIOBOOK
A Forgotten Poet
The Concord Diary

POETRY
Addendum Manifesto
Ghosts in the Machine
Laurel
Manifesto
Opus Thirty Three Bagatelles

PLAYS
The Two Gentlewomen of Dover
Who's Afraid of the Booker Prize?

†Winner of the 2018 Quagga Prize for Literary Fiction
††Winner of the 2015 Quagga Prize for Literary Fiction

That Was
Hugo Blythe MP

Peter Cowlam

AN Editions

AN Editions
aneditions.co.uk | editors@aneditions.co.uk
Copyright © 2025, Peter Cowlam

British Library Cataloguing in Publication Data
A catalogue record for this book is available from the British Library

Cover image curated by Philip Hall

ISBN 978-1-7384023-2-8

In memoriam Harry Greenberg, whose Highgate flat formed my model for Alaric's in Linden Gardens. Harry's was floor-to-ceiling stacked with books, so I did not need a public library. RIP

I am a lazy writer, for whom fiction is more easily made through hours of reflection than months of forensic research. The one flaw is reality, with its circus of celebrity, and dreary politicians getting in on the act. Hard it is for thoughtful beings, in a world of rolling news, to ignore how crass the arena is. But that makes the job of satire so much easier. And, I could not have told Lemuel's largely fictitious story without the dry disciplines more usually the tool of novelists. A book I became acquainted with was L. A. Naylor's *Judge for Yourself*, an investigation into the British judicial system, with its emphasis on notable miscarriages of justice, which I have drawn on. What fictions and inaccuracies are perpetrated hereafter – they're my own doing.

—**Peter Cowlam**

Foreword

Whether zilch or big, my quota of students wasn't fixed till a few days before the course began. At best, not many on that list left with a firmer philosophical grasp than when they arrived, and passed back out in a blissfully primitive state. I don't attribute this to failures communication-wise. The fact is mine was the university scene, and this was the first time I'd taught at an arts college (and probably the last). Let me try to be clear, as already there are problems with terminology. By 'zilch' I mean my last remaining candidate had decided to quit, and join the rest of my intake down in the gloom of the student bar. 'Big' on the other hand meant the biggest group I had was six.

Even that was disappointing, yet the truth was, whatever the numbers, Benbrook was never the panacea I'd looked forward to – a few hours a week teaching, and the chance to get away from London for days at a time. The drawback was, Benbrook's weren't exactly A-grade students, though they *were* all artists – a definition the institution had spent decades broadening out under the remorseless action of flatirons. One need only look to a recent alumni newsletter, which celebrates a near nominee – a rarity – for the Turner and other prizes. Another, I know, makes a hideous exhibition of herself anchoring children's daytime TV.

Those examples aside, the propaganda isn't easily maintained, for these are the lucky few (*few* is the operative word). Some way short of the glamour and the paycheques the newly enrolled expected, most of Benbrook's grads shuffle out through the college exit, reconciled to lesser fates. I personally cannot help equate those happy hopeful Benbrook student faces with the offices, shops and factories no workforce ever truly escapes, whatever the grim fantasies purveyed as television idyll, or by those wealthy and deranged enough to invest in the avant-garde.

And what of that avant-garde? Well, not all my students – such as I had – were involved in its installation works – objects amalgamating heavy industry with scrapbook marginalia. There existed a zany sub-reality called theatre, which due to its budget had learned to perfect what handbooks describe as the first three minutes. And there were writers, whose pen to paper had the brevity of postcards home. To grasp these limitations you had to backward glance the century we'd bidden our adieus to (with its global pyrotechnics) and try to understand how that had changed the way clever people viewed the world. It wasn't enough to practise, but to do so in the self-conscious awareness of the forces redefining our creations, even before they were birthed. These ranged from institutional epistemes, a padding on the edifice constructed for the use of those who governed, to mass aesthetics as a means of slavery, because most of society was held in subjection. One beheld the human horizon as a fluctuating *telos*, its traffic a process of semiotics, with any notion of the individual (rather than cult of personality) a sophisticated hoax.

My role in this inculcation traced wavy lines from Hegel's perfection of history, through Nietzsche's will to power, to Freud and his id, thence to Saussurean *langue* and *parole*, as a foreground for Lacan's symbolic order.

All simple enough when set out as that catalogue, yet even those students I was instructed to mark high, with firsts and upper seconds, could never get to grips with it. For example, how many times I said this: 'A rose is a rose is *not* a rose – it's an acoustic image.' And how many essays I marked where *only* a rose was this.

Benbrook had its compensations. Its academic departments had evolved from an earlier schoolhouse – a stone-built hamlet, kitted out with desks, and easels, and a newly enlightened teaching staff, all established at the height of the cocktail era. That had left today's very much larger campus with the same extensive rural views, awash with winding sheets of rain, or swathed in the mentholated breezes under watch of moorland cairns. My tenure, an abruptly truncated one, had for focus a tiny hub of lecture rooms, and in quieter hours – void of garrulous student life – opportunities to browse in the library and archive, both of which were handsomely stocked. I regret not getting to know the wider reach beyond, but the estate was vast. I did find time for the walks, a mixture of meadows, wooded rises, and acres of cultivated soil. These latter the

Benbrook Trust had always been insistent on, demanding good ecological principles – now and in perpetuity.

Given the improbability of teaching *anything*, my forays from the gloom of my lecture room, and into the blooms of its hinterland, took in Benbrook's inhabited outer edge. Here were houses constructed cottage-style, with timber roofing slates, and finished in the same grey render – decayed, cracked and peeling. They shared a line on either side of the road to college campus. The road narrowed to a track, then to a footpath, then existed notionally as the perimeter round a field. I assumed these charming houses were tenanted by Benbrook's long-term staff, or a selection of them, though I saw only *signs* of life, and never anyone actually there. These ghostly little indicators ranged from a child's bike, slung across a drive, its rear wheel spinning and aglitter in the sunshine, to washday whites hoisted above the fence line, and flapping loudly in the wind. Then strangely some of these properties *weren't* for living in at all, fronting instead obscure academic researches, none of which I encountered since (I noted one escutcheon in particular: The Data Institute of Scopophobia).

I didn't enjoy a vibrant social life, in part because of the distance I kept from Benbrook's teaching staff – colleagues I'd nothing in common with. I could never agree with them that human society was lacking in diversity where it thrived beyond the borderlines of Benbrook, or that as an arts pedant you had commented fully on Western civilisation, being one of those who'd placed a warehouse artefact – which of course I wasn't – into the latest conceptual art collection. These people anyway tended to congregate in the bars in the public performance venues – ancient, renovated architectures – old stone outcrops dotted round a grassy quad, and consisting of a theatre (very small, staging plays and cinema), a concert audit-orium (flagged and capacious, and excellent for chamber music), and a garden large enough for open-air Shakespeare – his comedies or romances put on yearly in July, by the Benbrook Players, an accomplished amateur group.

One acquaintance I *was* pleased to make I shall have to represent – for reasons the diary makes clear – only by his internet pseudonym – Trojan – Trojan a young London exile who headed up Benbrook's IT department. Some of the courses he ran were much more popular than mine, which I didn't resent at all, only because I couldn't overlook the usefulness of what he taught. Benbrook's students came automatically tuned to the information age (*if* nothing else), and most were open to tuition in the ins and outs of web design. There could be no better aid to the public projects drawn up as a module in Benbrook's first-degree courses. Trojan's stroll to work each day was from the campus domiciles just a few doors from the scopophobes, an end house of nightly beery soirées. The attraction was mostly a test match, camped on screen in his living room, and brought by satellite – not the only equipment his neighbours hadn't thought to invest in. Critically, an enlarged cubicle just off his kitchenette – looked in on by few other than me – was the partly secret place where, permanently at work, were bits of computer kit he'd fitted together himself. I counted screens, servers, lots of other junk, all vectored into weird-looking apparatus I personally wouldn't know what to do with. This hum of circuitry offered certain pastimes, involving, without much effort, hacking into major networks. One other diversion was intercepting email Benbrook's senior staff sent to one another endlessly. That alone offered insight into the marking system I'd been briefed to conform to.

It was here too at Trojan's place that I came across the internal newsletter that – one among other publications – the Right Honour-able Hugo Blythe MP had used to advertise for a new researcher. His wasn't the only application form I applied for and filled out, but it *was* the one I least anticipated ending in an interview (dramatic-ally it did). In any case, far from disinterested politically, wherever Labour (new or otherwise) pitched its tents, I followed on with bountiful reservations. As for Blythe's part in that new Messianic creed, all I knew was this – that he'd toured the estate on a blustery day in June. He was *our* minister – unencumbered by his entourage – gushingly received by the elders of Benbrook. What few hours he spent here were recorded in the local press – which I wasn't here to read – and ran to several pages on the Benbrook website (benbrook. ac.uk), which as Trojan, its facilitator, pointed out, was a litter of beaming photographs accompanied by sycophantic paragraphs penned by the resident poet. You can guess the heading: 'Hail to thee, Blythe spirit!' (innocent lines by Shelley turned into a tasteless rotating gif).

Yet in fact Blythe's interest wasn't the college at all, rather the music summer school that camped here year on year, a highpoint in Benbrook's calendar. This isn't necessarily chauvinism on my part. You can see for yourself on the appropriate web page the trio of admin staff, whose job was to lead the welcome committee. You can glean as I do – from the bemused smiles and apologetic handshakes – veiled indication of views not dissimilar to mine, untutored, alas, in the Brit Brat ethos. One stopping-off point was a whitewashed shippen, where a sculpted pile of lavatory seats awaited collection for an exhibition somewhere. I can envisage a diplomatic Hugo full of neutral appreciation, but with his thoughts on the summer school. The visiting conductor that year, who oversaw its operatic workshop, had placed *Ariadne auf Naxos* on the programme, and could boast that most of his musicians were still only teenagers.

That was the mixed perspective onto which I projected myself when Hugo offered me a choice of interview dates. I thought about it, then phoned an old academic friend – now at Surrey – whose books were in the Political Encounters series (Iconopoly Press). Hugo, he said, had entered politics fifteen or twenty years ago, having worked as editor of the political, cultural and literary journal *Risposta* – a voice vaguely of the left, muted with the onslaught of Margaret Thatcher's first administration, and the legacy *that* bequeathed. I found a tidy clutch of archive issues in the Benbrook library, and whiled away odd hours sampling his editorials, in no particular chronology. Ground covered ranged from the Glorious Revolution to Jethro Tull's seed drill, via Thomas Cranmer and the Book of Common Prayer. Another visit shed new light on John Harrison's chronometers, and that was followed by a second Harrison – Birtwistle – thence Spinoza's political philosophy, the Reform Bill of 1867, the Tolpuddle Martyrs, and Coleridge and Friedrich von Schlegel.

The interview took place on a grey, sporadically rainy day in mid-November, in a private room at the LSE. Hugo was taller than I imagined, stocky, hair a light straw colour, with no sign of thinning – a man somehow less than smartly dressed, despite the suit, which was a light charcoal, and baggy at the knees and elbows. His tie was silk, cerise, and neatly knotted. I'd heard him a lot lately on radio and TV, and was surprised at how quietly he spoke. What did we speak *about*? Well, two American poets – Anthony Hecht, John Ashbery – and before that a few words about my predecessor, who'd been mawkishly prone to sermonise if called on to write a speech when Hugo lacked the time. He had asked her to try and address that point, but all she'd done was transform any given text according to latest business methodology, producing an outcome that with minor changes to lineation, and the removal of punctuation, resembled computerised bulletisation. If ever *I* were called on, he was after something more lyrical, and didn't want to spend hours of his own redrafting.

'I've heard,' he went on, 'that you are, Alaric, opinionated.'

'Only where I *have* opinions.'

'Ah – you don't wade in where you don't….'

'Do you?'

'Sadly I often have to. When can you begin?'

Well yes, Benbrook *had* been a mistake, but there were drawbacks in what he proposed – its full-time basis, when halftime or less was what I wanted. Yet what was this timetable I'd managed to engineer, beyond a diminishing roll of students, who without the basics of education it was demoralising to try to teach anything….

'I'll start now,' I said, 'but I can't commit to more than a year.'

Hugo smiled affably at that. With a general election certain to be in May, we'd be lucky to survive into the next parliament.

I thought he was joking.

Diary

'Diary' isn't exactly it, though I remember thinking vaguely, having shaken hands with Hugo, and gone off in separate cabs – he towards Southampton Row, me to my flat off the Highgate Road – that here was a chance for an inside look at government. At the time I considered nothing so venal as selling to the press, as now I insist my hand has been forced. I am adamant, I never planned an exposé on the internecine state government ministers are prone to get into. In any event, the diary that evolved – from the marginalia my notebooks quickly filled with – is questionable as such, largely because the public document it accidentally became, and is due to become again (in a second coming, wholly premeditated by me), has been edited and added to retrospectively, with *precisely* the public in mind. That's my caveat anyway, and here is another: how attractive the semi-official memoir becomes when shaken and stirred as fiction.

With none of these schemes in mind, and having resigned, I extricated myself from all things Benbrook – including my short-term let on the moorland periphery. I did so as smoothly as I could, and spent the days tidying my upper-floor flat in Linden Gardens. I live at number 7, and have good territorial relations with my neighbour across the landing at number 8. On stepping out, day two of my return, on a planned visit somewhere, I mistook her for someone else, as expletives uncharacteristically hers echoed up the stairwell. I leaned over the banister and gazed into the varnished gloom, and made out at the foot of the stairs a yellow sleeve, and the flick of her hair as, irritably, she palmed it off her eyes. Her grief and agitation was a Christmas tree – half-price, she said, but too outspread and cumbersome – which for reasons I couldn't understand she was determined to plant in a bucket and decorate with tinsel in her living room.

'Emma,' I said, 'I'll give you a hand.'

A trail of pine needles down the few steps she'd ascended led to thicker deposits on the mat and across the hall, which she took a dustpan and brush to once we'd lugged the thing inside. I couldn't help think it was all so unlike her, and was as puzzled when, as I looked round, a small factory-load of greetings cards had been angled on her picture frames, and lined her ledges and other horizontal surfaces. What things had she failed to tell me, over the four or five years we'd exchanged domestic tales, or lent or borrowed flour, sugar, milk? I had seen no previous sign of enforced Christmas jollity, or the shop defilements of holiday time, or any such obedience to the calendar. And what was this? A new knick-knack adorning her television top, a stylised stable with crib and kings and the Virgin, and a sprinkle of gold glitter glued to its humble roof, and at its apex a star. Well – not, as it happened, the apotheosis I'd suspected. In a few hours her ten-year-old niece was due in from the south coast, and she'd got to meet her from her train at Charing Cross, and entertain her in the days before Christmas – all while the parents got divorced.

'Ah – I'm sorry to hear that.'

'Well that's marriage for you.' That blissful estate was one Emma, unlike her fool sister, had so far managed to avoid.

The niece when I met her – Charlotte – wore her hair in yellow ringlets, was shy, and a bit glum, and was addicted to daytime television, all at that moment a glut of Americana, spooned out in that prescriptive way the doctor has when his poisons he thinks are anodynes. I elicited a smile one afternoon over a mince pie, but got no more than that. It made me wonder in what sense Emma shared this failure, though I couldn't guess her reply, and felt only bewilderment when she called me back to the kitchen, and poured us a festive sherry. What followed was against her nature, as she put on her reading glasses, and standing before her freezer interrogated the cooking guidelines printed on a packet of burgers and a small plastic sack of oven chips.

I smiled at these eccentricities – Emma ferociously independent. I was pulled up at one other nod to convention, when hours later, and unexpectedly, I had a Christmas card from Hugo, which I now had to reciprocate. I scuttled off to the charity shops, where I pondered long and hard on what I should send him, in the end opting for moonlit fields under a pristine fall of snow, with a distant silhouette of yews round a village steeple.

December 20 Induction. My new place of work is a nondescript low-rise in Uttoxeter Street, which theoretically means a nice easy tube ride on the Northern Line, from Kentish Town to Charing Cross, and a leisurely stroll round Trafalgar Square. Hugo has asked me to announce myself no earlier than 9.30. I'm grateful for that, having missed the worst of the rush hour – which didn't exist at Benbrook. The receptionist, ensconced at an enormous desk in the foyer, felt moved to intone my name, with long equal weight to each of its five syllables, several times over, while with unnerving focus seeking facial clues from me.

'That's right. Alaric Casteele,' I said.

She checked against her diary. 'Ah yes.' She picked up her phone and spoke to Hugo. 'Do have a seat. He'll be down.'

I sank into the soft hinterland of one of two sofas, and scanned the low table positioned beside it, for anything undemanding – today's *Guardian*, lots of gardening magazines, a *National Geographic*, a withered copy of *The Stage*. I admit to a certain hesitation in rejecting the latter, though even then had failed to choose from the rest when Hugo breezed in, his jacket already discarded.

'Alaric, sorry! Phone calls, phone calls, phone calls.'

We shook hands then took the lift a floor up to the strategy room, a place festooned with dreary Christmas streamers, and not exactly hot with office activity. Two of its three desks were vacant, one of course being mine. At the third Avril (so she introduced herself) couldn't reboot her computer, and was phoning for an engineer. Hugo, as he led me to my intray, was summoned by his cell phone – its chime a revolving rococo introit – and patted all three trouser pockets searching for it. He recovered it only on retreating to his office. He stood for a moment in profile, framed by his doorjambs, portly at this remove, and prone to that first sign of a stoop, which collapsed to a hunch whenever he stood at the dispatch box.

I glanced up at the wall charts, of various hues, dominated by the department hierarchy – a sad mesh of lines, and a litter of discarded names, scored, erased or obliterated, with replacements hastily appended. I cannot vouch for its accuracy, and can't honestly say I garnered better information, but for what it's worth here is where I was – in the Department for Cult (as Hugo jokingly refers to it) – while at its summit, and not at all secure, sat the Right Honourable Hugo Blythe, MP. I can't recall all the tributaries, little mountain streams that branched off everywhere, into lakes and personalities I wasn't ever likely to meet, but here was the central thrust of that axis propping up his office, with Hugo beaming down. His foremost junior ministers were, in their correct hierarchical order: the Right Honourable Tamara Sorr, MP, whose responsibilities included, ominously, women's issues, and whose wide-ranging responsibility was for UK arts across all media (her populist brief was telegenic athletes, and other sports material), and below her was the Right Honourable Arabella Jury, MP, whose tendrils spread into e-government. The name etched beneath hers belonged to the Right Honourable Lord McGey of Merridoun, whose life was one of gentle rebukes, warmly voiced from the red plush in the Other Place.

There were more phone calls, and meetings, and not much chance for further contact, though Hugo – apologetic – pointed out he had asked Melissa, my predecessor, to cobble together some handover notes, which I'd find as a word-processed document on the computer sitting on my desk. That when I booted it had a Duron processor (850 megahertz), was running Microsoft Windows Millennium Edition, and had only 5.34 gigabytes of free space on the hard drive. Organisation of files and folders was shockingly inept, and imposing order was the first job. As things turned out – gradually – these handover notes took half an afternoon to find, though I stumbled on a good many impressions left by Melissa's footfalls through the department generally. The first thing I uncovered showed off her close association, only last month, with the Spoliation Advisory Panel – which in itself was a mould that I must fit. Here's what I mean. She waxed with a relish hard to describe on that body's latest recommendation, in this instance restitution of an artwork lost during the last Nazi era (she thought another Nazi era was shortly on its way, from across the Atlantic). Object in sight was a painting, part of the Pyrell Collection in Edinburgh, which according to expert purview had found its circuitous way into that city after illegal seizure from an auction house, in 1935. The picture was *L'heure du dîner*, attributed to an eighteenth-century artist called Saintard, and according to her, in a page-long preamble that boasted an enormous circulation list, it was 'morally' right, notwithstanding legal impediments, that the work be returned to its claimants, who remained anonymous. Melissa went on—

> We all know how crucial these questions of ownership are, especially those arising from Nazi depredations. The panel's recommendation must be the appropriate one, and certainly *I* am persuaded by their arguments. No one should need reminding: this government is wholly committed to the Washington Conference on Holocaust Era Assets, and in particular its declaration in December 1998, which addresses the issue of looted works of art.
>
> The public can only be perturbed that a museum in the British Isles lists a work identified as wrongfully parted from its owners. We can all take pride here in the UK of a record second to none when it comes to fighting fascism.

Yeah, well. The Nazis are one thing. My only question was, did the UK really have a record 'second to none' in the fight against not so latent elements on the far right?

I had nothing better to do, as was so often the case when working for Hugo, and saw immediately how hard it would be to avoid Melissa's pedantry. Here were her few less polished, unedited notes that dealt with Saintard himself, who was born in Paris in 1697, and died the same in 1776, famed for his still lifes and domestic scenes, said to be 'intimate in their realism'. He was also a portrait painter, who found his way into the Academy of Saint Luc in 1724, and the Royal Academy of Painting four years later. From there it's said – or Melissa said it's said – Saintard's career truly began, his projects ranging from scenes of family life, to half-figure paintings – usually of youngish men and women either working or at leisure. Louis XV is popularly quoted as having paid 1,800 livres each for two in this series, products that had ceased to imitate the rusticity of Louis Le Nain, an earlier exemplar. Melissa has the critic's vocabulary: 'The manners are softened. The models are rid of that austere peasantry marked by Le Nain the precursor. The housewives are simply and neatly attired, and communicate an orderliness you see also in the houses where they live. They offer intimacy, a sense of fellowship, an unassuming domesticity, so highly valued by a later age of connoisseurs…' – as I cannot help think Melissa has missed – or probably now has found – her true vocation.

Altogether a dull first day at work.

December 21 A bleary-eyed Avril explains – over her first morning coffee – how her engineer was forced to work into the evening, having arrived late yesterday afternoon, his first job reformatting her hard drive, followed by the laborious process of reinstalling whatever software she uses, not to say adding back any data she's been prudent enough to save offline. I don't know what to make of Avril. I gather she researches for Tamara, but isn't at all forthcoming about what that research is exactly. She's young, but frumpy (plain drabs etc., Spartan with her makeup), so I did not expect her pale, marmoreal exterior to register what raptures it did – sudden snorts and plosives, let loose mid-flight – on testing out her newly refurbished PC. Her most earnest check was downloading yesterday's news off the internet, having paused at a Sunday premiere, where she shared in its drool over the graceless celebrity its publicity thrust came gift-wrapped with. Its stills and video clips raised streaks of pink in Avril's cheeks. Touchingly, a few brief words on a de la Renta gown she scrolled off-screen the moment I stepped across neutral office ground to see what it was. She replaced it by a member of the Opposition brandishing his copy of *Nineteen Eighty-Four*, in protest at government plans for identity cards, for such were the depths of the Tory backbench.

After these and other skirmishes she removed herself for most of the afternoon, returning sporadically to type up notes from meetings, but remained otherwise uncommunicative. The high point of my day was a call put in from the lower echelons of IT, to tell me an email address had now been allocated – alariccasteele@cult.gov.uk (my little joke).

'We'll send someone down to set the thing up.'

'Read over the details and *I'll* set it up.'

'I'm afraid for security reasons that's quite impossible.'

'I see.'

By four there was still no sign of Hugo, and nor did he phone, so I stuffed a few papers into my case and meandered back to Highgate.

I'd been back for half an hour when Emma's long, slow, insistent, nevertheless genteel little rap at the door interrupted my afternoon wash and shave. I put my shirt back on and buttoned up, and saw, when I unlatched the door, that hers at number 8 remained wide open. Decoded that meant 'do not ask me in'. A glance into the dusky lamplight slanting across her hall confirmed it. Unusually, lines were graven on her face, reminding me how little that did for her looks – which were plain, scholarly, but interesting – and always at their worst when she frowned or furrowed her brow. Of course I *knew* how she hated asking favours, but irksome as it was she got to the point. She'd had a surprise invitation for tomorrow night, which in any other guise would not have been hard to turn down. But there'd been more than a hint, in the way it was couched, at something to her advantage, and of course what mattered was her career. Short notice as it was, someone would need to keep an eye on Charlotte.

'You're asking *me*? Is that wise?'

'Alaric, whatever do you mean?'

'The girl hardly speaks – not at all to me.'

'She's shy.' That, as a girlish trait, was something Emma had thought about. 'Come round for dinner. Let Charlotte get to know you,' the 'you' being an Alaric distinct from the grunts and footfalls leaden across his landing. I couldn't see it as enough to put the girl at her ease, but Emma meant it.

'Only an hour,' I said. 'I'm crammed full of paperwork.'

'Appreciated, Al.'

I changed into lined cotton trousers, a newly laundered shirt, and – Emma sparing with her central heating – a brightly coloured woollen cardigan. I tapped on the door and was ushered in shortly after seven. Perhaps predictably I found Charlotte, once it was clear I *had* crossed the threshold, sunning herself with awful resolution in the rays of Emma's TV – a mind caught young and malleable in the wooden dictates of English adult life lived soap-opera-style. I managed to prise her away while Emma prepared, cooked and drained the pasta, but only as far as the computer. There, only slightly more animated, Charlotte showed me the batch of CD games she'd brought. I offered effortless curiosity, and no scepticism at all at the ones labelled educational, geared to the national curriculum. But I couldn't help think that if all communication stood to be deferred through third-party devices, tomorrow wouldn't be fun.

I stepped into a kitchen full of steam, where Emma had spooned an olive and pine-nut sauce into a bowl of cannelloni, which, when served, Charlotte prodded round her plate without enthusiasm.

Glad to get home to my papers.

December 22 A test email from IT, requesting a response, was followed by a flood from all sorts of people everywhere. I found this astonishing, given the age of my email address – a newborn, barely a day old. I hovered on the delete key, then pasted a small sample into the ragbag of text I'd begun to accumulate on a day-to-day basis – for a closer look another day (or so my thinking ran). I asked, did I really have to consider the repeated questions my correspondents all wanted answers to? Some were private individuals, with nothing better to do, and of course I ignored them. The vast majority prowled the connecting labyrinths fusing mine with other political empires. Said an AH, from the tartan depths of the Scottish Office, commenting on that sodden explosion arising over ID cards: was this a media issue – and not *only* to do with civil liberties – now that the BBC had participated in piloting biometric data? A Michael B from Education asked, on the right to free speech: was this a concept we no longer defended? He cited violent protests in the Midlands that had led to a repertory theatre cancelling one of its runs. Well, Michael B, search me. Then again a humble clerk in the Home Office couldn't say how relieved she felt that a plan to falsify a cannonball, and pass it off as originating with the shipwrecked *Mary Rose* – or Henry VIII's flagship – had been thwarted, and wouldn't after all be auctioned on the internet. (Phew!)

Avril, who was more than usually remote, at last warned me not to make plans for this afternoon, her advice prompted when a spindly peon, with a ragged-looking goatee – an indentured slave somewhere on the supply line to the House of Windsor – delivered two dozen crates of cheap, and probably repugnant wine, and beer brewed and canned in a rain-swept city distant in the north. Our office do – or rather its deluge of personnel – started at half-past two, when loud, garrulous people, pink from wheezing into party blowers, or tipsy from other visits made *en route*, filled our crowded space – first with industrial chat, then with a cumulus of fag smoke.

I crossed the room and opened the windows, but on retracing steps found my desk and chair perch to a trio from Environment, Food and Rural Affairs, guffawing over the foxhunt ban. This wasn't my conversation. I inspected – and finally rejected – all that sad vino, and poured myself a plastic cup of beer. Perhaps due to the innocence some have in new surroundings, I was prey to atrocious conversations I might have avoided otherwise. An attractive woman half my age expressed her opinion that party colours necessarily planted themselves as much with the politics of public art as with any other manifesto issue. I did not have her capacity for hellish descents, and said only of a recent showing she'd attended – in the cold and gore of a slaughterhouse – that this was rather the perversion of serious aesthetics.

'That I can't imagine is the kind of thing your boss would say.'

'Hugo?'

'*Or* Tamara.'

'Tamara I haven't met.'

'They wouldn't approve.'

'I am just the right corrective then.'

This and other pointless scrapes so teetered on the brink of farce I was tempted to lock up my desk and retire for the day, and might have done so but for certain scraps of things I overheard – someone telling someone else that Hugo was on his way. In fact Tamara preceded him, by half an hour, a waifish imitation of that other presence I knew – her screen or news-clip aura. Truth was, that preparation for the camera turned her into someone less fatigued, whose unveiling before us, in the fluorescence of office life, was the pale luminescence of her flesh, a figure unnaturally slim, and a neck wrinkled and wizened past her fifty-odd years. One noted the toothy coal seam when – as she often did – she smiled or enunciated.

Avril promised to introduce me, and succeeded, eventually, once she'd engineered a mazy little path through the eager social groupings hanging on her boss's every word. We shook hands. Hugo, she said, had told her such a lot about me. That I doubted, but nevertheless played to her charade. Hugo we agreed was a thoughtful sort of man, if not at this stage easy to pin down. In his absence, she said, a valuable piece of professional advice was to write down absolutely everything, and likewise record the merest shred of written material other people sent to me.

'I'll try to remember that,' I said. [How am I doing, Tamara?]

She turned and spoke to Avril before she left, their coded, loaded exchange shockingly impolite in its spiral of confidentialities, for which I stood aside and watched. Then abruptly the minister disposed of her tomato juice, and with a nod only in my direction set off for her waiting car. Hugo – a peach tie and shiny suit, roomy at the knees and elbows – replaced her almost immediately, a revised cue as now those same hordes vied for *his* attention.

His mood was relaxed, warm even. His features, never fixed for long, exploded into bright sunny beams, accompanied by an apologetic handshake, so soon as I'd parted the throngs and got him in conversation – regrets on his part, and a blur of explanations as to why these past few days he'd had to abandon me.

'No worries, Hugo.'

'I'm so glad. You are er finding your way?'

I told him Melissa's handover notes were a complicated labyrinth of files and folders arced across my disc system, and that the process of reorganisation into a structure more attuned to my methods was under way. 'Oh, and by the way – I've got an email address.'

That, given the strange impossibility of keeping other folk at bay, was as far as we got, though he did ask what I was doing for supper. By chance we didn't live far apart, and I was about to suggest a place – a bistro famed for its garlic sauce – but remembered Charlotte, and so put it off for another night.

'I'll catch you tomorrow.'

'There's an *outside* chance.'

I left as the party had reached its last desperate throes, and was home early. Shortly after five I was followed up the stairs by Charlotte and her aunt, who'd had a fractious afternoon in Oxford Street, and couldn't coordinate their parcels and the door key – or anyway not without Emma's fairy curses. I stumbled in at eight, at that precise moment when Emma had zipped herself into her evening gown, and but for one strand persistently falling loose wore an elegant coiffure, her hair bunched to the crown. I'm afraid it was never something I could help with, but fortunately Charlotte, pyjamaed and sweetly fragrant from her bath, took the initiative.

I managed to keep her, when Emma had gone, away from the TV listings, and asked her to fetch whatever books she'd brought. She rummaged in her room and produced *one* – in large picture format, with a substantial text. Its jacket blurb – penned for the assiduous parent – told how this author I now thought better of orating was buoyed by a string of awards. A brief résumé encapsulated text and illustrations, centred on a child whose father dies, one of life's grey equations you'd have thought unresolved, even in the didactics of a book designer's backflap, in this case adamant that 'how to grieve' was something children 'could be taught'.

'This is fine,' I said to Charlotte, 'but what do you read for pleasure?'

She looked at me curiously. 'Pleasure?'

I made no further comment, but scanned Emma's shelves in search of something – anything – a little less saturnine. That became an exercise, as half a dozen books to do with Emma's profession (her profession was archaeology) passed through my hands. One in particular caught my eye, whose last in its trio of authors was a name that Emma mentioned often, and was someone she probably knew. I found it wedged horizontally and bookmarked at an assortment of monochrome photos, which grouped as a narrative objects of votive offering, detritus from a sewage pit, and a bag of shaman's stones. No good for Charlotte, clearly, who with her thumb in her mouth was staring up, perplexed. I tiptoed up to the two upper shelves, but all *they* offered – which was also not a surprise – was Emma's most venerated feminists. I was about to head back across to number 7 when I found, in a saving cornucopia adjacent to the hearth, an old but sturdy Lewis Carroll.

I cannot tell you with what desperation my triumph evaporated, when after only a few sentences Charlotte was gazing as blankly as the blank TV gazing back.

December 23 News is thin, this close to Christmas. I say that because this morning, at breakfast time, I heard Tamara suffer rebukes on Radio 4, by an interviewer not deterred at the ghostly phone connection over which the two conversed. Topic was the theft of dozens of antique maps from the National Library in Wales, while the thief – a man in the vortex of gambling debts – seemed to both these women almost incidental. Tamara, coaxed from her usual generalities, finally gave in to a battery of probes, and meant to say something like: if larceny on so habitual a scale had gone unchallenged for so incredibly long, then of course that was all in the devious circuits of thievery (which was in itself circuitous).

I was already late for work, so switched off and didn't catch the conclusion. That I got from Avril, who as ever was first in the office. According to her – who probably rose at dawn and read every conceivable newspaper – 105 maps were missing, though only 50 the thief admitted to. These and other points had so far been kept from public discussion, because the authorities couldn't bear the embarrassment, with library security not as it should be. More alarming than that, I couldn't tell from Avril's look and tone if her amused giggles *were* what they seemed, or part of a dangerous ethics only *I* saw manifesting as snorts of abhorrence.

At last I heard from Hugo, who phoned – from a train to Birmingham. He battled to tell me, his strained if cheery banter interrupted by a loss of signal several times, that he expected to be back later that afternoon. I put it to him politely that were I given access to his diary, certain ideals in communication stood to be achieved. Somehow the reply invoked visions of myself as a dreamy pipe-smoker, dwelling in a distant Utopia, one of those nations he certainly liked to think about, but only as an emollient. At the moment his life was event- and not diary-driven.

'Well never mind,' I said. 'There's plenty I can do here.'

I returned to Melissa's paper world of espionage, and found in her folder marked 'People and Organisations' two others, colour coded red and green. In the latter were duplicated emails, bills and flyers and other things she'd scanned, whose origin was persons or groups she'd decided Hugo ought to know about, or meet. These typically were women big in community arts and education, whose quest was funding, or whose spleen needed written outlets in cases where they'd tried for that and failed. Her red bloc on the other hand was a cordon on people Hugo was, and must remain, inaccessible to – not exclusively men, yet no man in this corral could cross to his counterparts in green. Here among those interdicted I came across this, of a grandiloquence I would meet again, which outdid even mine—

Hugo. It is now almost half the year's calendar since, as a key voter in your electorate – a man who lives the narratives you force on the rest of us – I entrusted my latest cargo to the whims of your post sack. These modest gifts aren't more than a subtext – in my case the product of someone who dares to raise his pen against the tide of louder voices everywhere. Haven't you read it by now (a pocketbook of poems, called *Razor Manifesto*)? Or is this gaping silence how New Labour likes to honour its poets?

Yours, Robert

The response came *not* from Hugo—

Dear Mr Hailer,

Thank you for your email addressed to Hugo Blythe. As I am sure you can appreciate, the minister receives so much correspondence it is not always possible for him to respond personally. Your email has therefore been passed to me, and I have been asked to reply.
	I have checked our tracking system and it would seem your collection of poems, *Razor Manifesto*, was not received by this department, and therefore was not passed on to the minister. If it *were* here, I assure you we certainly would have replied. I am sorry your efforts to bring your poems to the minister's attention were not successful.

Melissa Dupliss (Arts Policy)

In my mind this raised perplexing questions as to the flow of information in and out of the department, or more important who controlled the various stages in that process. Casually, I put these points to Avril, who told me – in a disdainful tone it did no good to try to penetrate – that we didn't concern ourselves with every envelope or paperclip.
	Gagged as he was, a final riposte went to Robert Hailer (not a name I knew till then), in whose defiant tone one reads his emasculation as complete—

Dear Ms Dupliss,

Odd that our English Hermes, glossed in a Post Office stripe, couldn't deliver to you in Uttoxeter Street, but did succeed with the book's dedicatee, a Mr Tony Benn, who replied promptly. That old Leveller also receives a great bulk of mail every day.

Are they to tempt me with defection, these decisions you make, even when viewed through the prisms of literary art (diminished, I own, in an era of instant gratification)? Or would you say a want of popular political engagement only incubates a parallel disease afflicting all arts endeavours everywhere? Is *that* the malady?

Yours, Robert Hailer

Ms Dupliss added nothing to this, and given the age of their correspondence there was little I could do.

Got home early again, about four o'clock. With a better chance of getting work done here, I began the laborious task of purging the dead accumulated megabytes the drives of my own computer had spawned, much of it to do with Benbrook (a ruthless scythe I took to it). Outside, a solidifying darkness had replaced the blue vapours and lateness of the afternoon. At last I took a break. A little restless, I drew the curtains. I put the kettle on. From the kitchen I cannot usually hear the door, but a loud knock – added to the softer one I'd missed – was unmistakably Emma's. She introduced her younger sister Anna – Charlotte's single parent – a brunette an inch or two shorter than her sibling, a youngish woman fuller in the face, and physically more exuberant, if less so intellectually. She'd be here – at number 8 – over the bank holiday.

'Thanks for babysitting Charlotte.'

'Have a cup of tea.'

They stepped inside, long enough to hand me something Christmas-wrapped from Anna. I saw from its shape what it was approximately, spirits or other liquor, still in its cylindrical packing, trussed in a reflective, foxy paper, and tagged with a note.

'You're busy, Al.' Both glanced across at the computer, and beside it my open briefcase.

'That's only work….'

'Al's new boss is a government minister.'

'Exciting!'

'Actually it's deadly routine.'

I turned to the computer, and casually scrolled through my notes, perturbed and shocked at how flawed by its gossip the job was turning out to be, all eyes having fallen on my entry for December 20,

Only last month the Spoliation Advisory Panel…

and again the 21st,

I don't know what to make of Avril…

and there were others from yesterday, which I didn't allow us to dwell on.

Spent a few more hours after they'd gone adding, changing, excising. Went to bed late – not tired, but thoughtful. Could somehow still trace Anna's perfume.

December 24 An unspectacular end to the working year, beginning with a hopeless muddle for change, and a missed train in consequence, and threatening to peter out midday-ish, all instruments of commerce eerily quiescent under the falls of paperwork, an office kind of snow. No phone, no email. Avril made modest work of lunch, then, having put on her coat, summoned effortless diplomacy in wishing me a pleasant yule. I followed her example, but held back at the bustle for transport, and instead trod the streets – me in my long black coat – half looking out for passing cabs. By what mishap I cannot say, and not perhaps without premeditation, I meandered into a bookshop, having stood outside under the beams of its literati – photographic portraits vying with one another's profiles, all for the tinselled upper reaches of its window display. Inside, I couldn't find much by Robert Hailer – his *Razor Manifesto* nowhere in the poetry section – though I came away with one other slim collection of his verse, published as long ago as 1991, by Exe University Press.

I made no plans, and at home rather than skim through Hailer's paperback – which I left on the kitchen table, with the debris of my breakfast things – I found another way of wasting time, the clock plodding from four o'clock to seven. I schemed about the girl next door, with its too many complications, I told myself. The problem resolved itself when suddenly Hugo phoned, landline-to-landline, with papers he'd got at his house, which he wanted to go through – with me. His address was a plain, bow-fronted terrace in a street in Kentish Town, which when I checked the A to Z was a brisk walk, not too far. What to take with me? Anna's gift from yesterday I'd stripped away as far as the cardboard tube, and with solemnity had weighed but not yet opened. It was a twelve-year-old Glenfiddich. I tucked it in my briefcase, and headed off.

I got there as Hugo was seeing out through his hallway a forlorn-looking, wiry-haired youth – no more than. After passing introductions I was left to myself, alone in the tiny living room, with its listless décor – walls a wash of maroon, each with a spreading fan of pearls, their source a set of uplighters, opaque and oyster-shell in shape. A small, squarish settee, and single matching chair, were thinly upholstered – fronds and leaves and stems on a background blossom pink. The curtains were opulent, while the carpet defiantly was not. His books, and his papers, and a vanload of weekend supplements, all cohabited without ill will on something self-assembly – as did a TV with VCR. These latter two appliances were alive, but temporarily framed in silence, their present, ghoulish output semi-stilled, Hugo having stabbed at the pause button. I could just about make out, in the elastic distensions horizontal across the screen, the departing head and torso of someone – a male, I felt sure – reclining on a single-seater couch. No sign of Hugo yet, who'd enlighten me. With the front door still open, funnel to all passing street noise, he and his caller stood in the porch, completing their business – a series of chopped-up sentences, and a hum of interjections I made no sense of. Presently the front door closed, and his visitor – one of Hugo's foot soldiers, trusted with important work at constituency HQ – trotted out to his little blue Fiat parked across the street, a few doors up.

Hugo breezed in, the hearty welcome that had formed on his lips already receding on the instant he'd opened his mouth, about to speak. That was down to me, our night's work stalling a second time, or rather down to my frozen stance before that flicker from his television set.

'Ah yes, *that*,' he said.

He groped in the well of his settee and in a wedge between its cushions put his hand on the TV/VCR remote, old, huge and cumbersome, and with a flourish pointed it. The tape whirred slowly into action, in a splurge of sound, harness to that disintegrating image bit by bit reassembling itself. I could not guess on what unwholesome hour, nights past, Hugo had set the recorder running, though the format was familiar: arts guru, interviewed by other arts guru, two members of the only species able to educate the after-midnight masses. With what awful majesty the show's host remained off camera, intercepting the bulk of important points with fortifying grunts, or a giggle of innuendoes. Blagueur resolutely in shot wore a jazzed-up suit with a ponceau tie, and with a cheery pessimism endemic to his trade told us how wholesome everything really was. His proposition: we need to dismiss the *sanctity* of Johann Sebastian, for were he operating now, among the plastic ornaments of *our* decades, he was bound to be scoring flaccid tunes for boy bands. 'Well absolutely,' says she with her own show at last, but still out of shot.

Said Hugo, with his jacket off, and the sleeves of his shirt rolled up: 'Interesting notion....'

'Um.'

He pressed, paused, and pressed again the fast-forward button, in the uncertainty of something sought that couldn't be found. He gave up finally and turned the TV off. (And so, my friends, to business.)

A small gate-leg table at the window, where the bay was damp and chilly, Hugo had spread with the papers he wanted us to go through – all a lot less daunting than it looked. I slung my coat across the settee, prepared for a longer night than actually occurred, and having so resigned myself produced Anna's bottle of Glenfiddich, whose neck, as I slipped it from its cardboard sheath, I didn't expect to find beribboned, in an attractive combination of Prussian blue and gold. I explained what I thought it meant, less convinced myself than was Hugo, who obliged nevertheless with an ice trough, and two tiny Highland jugs. In the glow of all that anaesthetic, work commenced. Approximately half a bottle later, and lots of action points for me, I asked if the name Robert Hailer meant much to him at all.

'Ah yes, Hailer.' Would he or would he not censor from his memoirs – a figment of his future I alone had notice of – certain impressions Hailer had stamped on the '97 hustings? (that was the question, Al). He recalled how that particular voter, with mild intent that rapidly turned to bile, trailed everywhere after him out on the stump, his questions framed in the spirit of critique, but with menace. For his *coup de théâtre* he chose the intimate surroundings of University College School – in whose theatre Hugo might plausibly assume that those he addressed were friends. Hailer reiterated some of those points he'd already uttered many times before, in town or market squares, or in indoor assemblies. Why were there not more poets in the House of Lords? As ever Hugo dealt with that by promising to investigate canonisation procedures, with Hailer – at that time a name known to him through the pages of *Oxenford Poets* – a borderline candidate. Fame at last, Robert. Very well, then – what about the corrupting advance system operated by all the UK's leading publishers, as it favoured names over content, and the sons of *someone*?

Yes – what about that?

Wasn't it a scandal?

Quite possibly – yet government was notoriously counter-productive when it interfered with market forces.

So to Hailer's riposte, delivered *sans-culotte*, from out where he lived on the outskirts of rebellion: you couldn't be consistent in *that* view *and* support the principle of Arts Council funding, and if Hailer was less than familiar with the internal structure of that public body, he was nevertheless clear it was government meddling with both aesthetics *and* the market. Did that not show – in whatever administration – that a preference for what or who received financial aid certainly did exist?

Point taken. Therefore if, as Hugo anticipated, New Labour got elected, he personally undertook to look at how that leviathan worked.

Said Hailer: 'I'll hold you to that.'

'Sounds quite a fiery character,' I said.

'He is after all a poet.'

I carefully re-screwed the lid on the Glenfiddich, and with ballpoint poised ran swiftly through the remaining wodge of paper. Hugo was tired, and puffy round the eyes, and with a weariness I hadn't seen in him before he closed to the first of our conclusions. That being a gainfully recycled, tatty-looking folder, its shade a faded mustard, stuffed with paperwork he briefed me to follow up on. Yet, I would not at that stage return *it* – or the Glenfiddich – to the safety of my briefcase, still having doubts as to 1997 as his last exchanged *touché* with Robert Hailer.

'Let me think a bit,' he said.

With a thud and a purling of pipes the central heating, hot and oppressive till then, completed its nightly cycle, a perturbation that for an instant interfered with his reflections. Then, a marvel of spontaneity, it occurred to him that Hailer had probably moved onto someone else's patch. How so, Hugo? Well, since I asked, he couldn't recall those Haileresque harangues from the 2001 campaign, and he'd never seen him at one of his Saturday surgeries. Could that be, Hugo, that as government isn't like opposition, voter scepticism gives up finally, bedumbed? Quite possibly, though he did remember – from he knew not how many aeons ago – Hailer's brush with certain feminist counterparts, reported with aplomb in one of the weekend supplements, as I'd find on raking through his shelves.

'I'll pour another drink,' I said. '*You* look.'

'Why is this important?'

'It's valuable entertainment.'

Incredibly he found said article, so that it, or rather the publication it appeared in, joined those other bits and pieces in my bag. I put on my coat and said goodnight, and tottered out – a little uncertainly – still bewitched by the liquor on my lips, whose vapours rose in plumes. I looked, and couldn't see a cab, so buttoned my coat and marched.

December 25 A late start – eleven. For breakfast I lightly browned a slice of toast, and prepared a cafetière (fair-trade coffee alleged). For lunch I planned a bowl of lentil soup, and for dinner scrambled egg and anchovies, with a square of bread and butter.

Sadly these good intentions went awry. At shortly after one o'clock Emma – rather than stride across the landing – looked up the lone Casteele in her local directory, and phoned. After opening pleasantries, followed by an awkward pause, and further hesitations, she told me frankly how sweet with melancholy her sister Anna felt, having seen inside my house – that's to say a place void of Christmas tack. I have an elegant mahogany clock on my mantelpiece, and there's a giltwood pier-glass centred on the chimneybreast above it, and this is flanked on either side by the handful of cards I haven't thrown away – their secret chemistry a new street or email address written in the postscript.

'What she really wants to know is what you've planned for Christmas lunch.' I imagined the gravity these words were uttered with, not at all matched by the awkwardness Anna – and possibly Charlotte too – saw etched in her face.

'Nice of you to call. A happy Christmas, all. I have no special plans.'

'Oh in that case why not come over…?'

It was hard to say no, and so – as I took my time – I plucked an Argentine red, and a Chardonnay also from the south, from the remote ceiling heights up on the rack, and slipped across to number 8, where – as I might have anticipated – Charlotte was snugly cushioned, awaiting her daily deathly foam of TV inculcation. The two sisters had decamped to the kitchen, a long time ago, with the door ajar, their coven totalling three once Emma – her face flushed with oven heat – had ushered me inside. I put down my bottles, then folded arms at the heavy table as, with a swagger, and with wonderful precision, Anna uncorked the red. So preoccupied, one gauged with what expertise she applied and wore her makeup. Where just a day or two ago I had placed her mid-to-late-thirties, I now put her well into her forties – not much younger than I was, probably. These unlikely contemplations were not allowed to last. Symbolic feasts are borne on a train of practicalities, and it was my job to tilt the meat tray, while Emma – she having driven out to the Chiltern Hills to buy it – began to baste a rib of beef, now out on the hob and removed from under its foil.

Anna had her doubts, with Emma not used to home cooking on a friends or family scale. The cut of meat was fit for double our quota of adults. The conversation didn't stick with that, as somehow we arrived at a bit beyond mere pleasantries. I said no, I'd never married. The natural consequence of that was offspring, and that had no appeal to persons shod for hermetic mental disciplines. A glance round the doorjamb into the living room, awash with that broadcast corrosion children are turned into consumers with, emphasised my point. So therefore for Anna the only remaining question was why I wasn't spending Christmas with my parents.

There was sadness in that explanation too, since both had died, over twenty-five years ago, in a road accident, for which I was partly responsible. The culmination of a laborious journey was a long stretch of road out of West Malling, *en route* to Hadlow where they lived, having hours before farewelled me in Manchester, where I'd almost completed my masters. Officially my father had fallen asleep at the wheel, but *I'm* not convinced (he strayed into the path of a delivery truck, whose driver slewed his cab at just such an angle that *he* survived).

What memories. My father could infuriate by his evenness of manner, a man cloaked in an austere calm you could not identify in the previous generation, ontogenetically or otherwise. Whatever the genes swimming in our pool, they weren't common property. Physically I resembled him, and that made our diametric oppositions hard to understand – to the point that his paternal equanimity, to me, was an artificial construct. Perhaps only *I* thought it, but that made his presence shallow in its exterior – a falsity tragic in its outcome for me. What persists is an injury I cannot remedy, because the one chance I saw for that was extinguished once the bodies were bagged and the wreckage swept away. From what was left, all I can allow myself, in how I remember him, is a list that reads like passport attributes, adding up to not very much. He didn't go grey. He did not lose his hair. He stayed lean throughout his life without troubling with exercise, and he wasn't communicative. All this remained his constant even under duress, which all of us suffered mostly during my adolescence (I don't mention other protracted disorders that have been affective since). I don't know but can guess that his success in what he did didn't give rise to usual career delusions. He was first to know – as I certainly know – that what we are is an indefinite interlock of activities, accidents, events, not untouched by luck. *His* luck was to run his own publishing firm, which specialised in law – books for corporate lawyers. I tried to keep the business on through some of the people he employed, but couldn't trust them – and anyway all exchanges were done by phone from Manchester. In the end it was easier to sell, which I did – to one of the conglomerates. I also sold the house in Hadlow, though I kept the gîte in Brittany, as I did also the investments – all this while I plodded on with my masters. I thought hard once that was over, deciding not, as I'd previously planned, to carry on and do my doctorate. (Still haven't done it.)

How much of this was more than private introspection? Well, only the gîte, which I planned for three or four times a year, with a first trip pencilled in for early spring. Anna, forced to agree that despite her sibling auguries, the joint of beef was worth that drive to the Chilterns, mused that a trip to northern France – or ideally a jet south into the sun – was something she'd thought about for Charlotte and herself (wistfully, as things turned out, and after everything they'd been through). I weighed this information carefully, as we pulled our crackers and put on our party hats.

'I can lend you the keys,' I said.

She stalled. Agonised, I understood she was short of funds, and changed the subject. Then the point was lost when, late in the afternoon, Charlotte was made to show me her presents – some stock digital gadgetry, and one or two books as dry and uninspired as the one I'd opted not to read on Wednesday night.

December 26 I don't feel the compulsion I thought I might to gather every scrap of news, which, anyway, given present circumstances, is likely to end in problems. I gave up on my morning paper years ago, tired at its expertise, but worse than that – after lacklustre efforts – failed to replace it, by *anything* on offer, internet, broadsheet, tabloid. I listen to the radio, but have to switch it off when – too much for dwellers at sea level – the mountaineering ethos prized of the corporation claims some latest summit lost to the clouds, too elevated in its moral tones. But I do know this: that the Ukraine is poised to elect its new president after mass protests over vote-rigging; that a Russian cargo craft laden with vital supplies has docked with the international space station; and that the Pope in his Christmas address cannot ignore that the world we have made is endless in its conflict. Through conflict we define ourselves.

That dinner I didn't have yesterday I had for breakfast today, a poached egg and anchovies on toast. I was confident I wouldn't be disturbed, and sat at my chair in the window, where I emptied of its content Hugo's file – papers, papers, papers. Immediately the phone rang. I gazed across the street and left it to the answer machine, and saw Emma buttoning up her coat, and with great purpose striding for the Highgate Road.

No matter. I shuffled my papers, and settled for a batch not so randomly chosen. Propped by that very nice Glenfiddich, Hugo and

I had talked and guffawed over a man called Alan Baines, a good-hearted, dishevelled, backbench, old-style Labour MP, blessed with a safe seat distant in the north. Baines had misconstrued, and perhaps wilfully, the era of massaged news, which had opened him to most kinds of no-through road. A good example was Baines's public outrage at the UK's depleted fishing industries. He invited in the press. Local TV also turned up, sensing a reet good filler for its brush with teatime current affairs. Baines's chosen venue was an Old Street chip shop ('Lived 'ere fer years'), where he demolished, on camera, an enormous haddock supper – with salt, vinegar, tartare sauce – and explained some rudiments of economics, which the EU had lost sight of.

In more recent times his not so favourite tabloid had resurrected dependable mythologies, and as part of that project 'restated' his views on asylum and immigration. Upshot was, the hapless Alan Baines MP had strayed too close to one of those pocket devices, recording *everything*. Remarks he'd made were *re*made, as a kind of common-sense xenophobia. Pointless were his protests.

That and other press debacles prompted memos, emails – a swirl of directives – whose encapsulating wisdom came from the top tent, telling us whatever the circumstance we on the ground ought never to say what we think. 'Remember, we approach each important challenge with a well-meaning all-inclusiveness.' Baines said openly he could not agree that politics was a synonym for concealing what you thought, and carried on with another scheme he'd got. That took him, when the House was sitting, on a tour of the lobbies, corridors, bars and tearooms, canvassing for names, which with schoolboy gusto he added to his list of no votes (and possible nos if not decided), as he looked ahead to the EU referendum (whenever that might be). One of many rumours currently circulating put Hugo's name indelibly on that list, which if true was an act of treason likely to place him on another roll – i.e., the casualties' – in the next reshuffle.

Hugo denied any such liaison, and told me in confidence this and other scare tactics was the work of his enemies. I took it on trust, unable to coax him – however vague – into stating or guessing at who those enemies were. (They're known to me now all right.) Nor did Hugo counter these dangerous eddies against him – gossip in all its vortices – when it was true he'd spent a lot of time with Baines, a point I pressed him on until I got an explanation. He said this – that Baines and others like him, if unimpressed by the constitution's wording, weren't necessarily Eurosceptic. There was, behind his bluff façade, a child of an older demotic steeped in political unrest. Hugo found the right opposing factor to those necessary texts, scholarly tomes under ceaseless revision, hard dry tablets of Anglo-Saxon social life, which he read, he said, with practical insight, and an eye to the parallels Baines would insist still existed – Baines who knew his Lollards, Diggers and Chartists.

It was my difficult task to draft a succinct, incisive statement Hugo could rehearse, the end being, under force of interrogation, that he'd the right words to distance himself from the Europhobic mob. I took up my pen and pad, and wrote—

I have never at any time held the view that…

and tried again…

No. I certainly don't subscribe…

…and again,

Let me say in passing…

…and for the moment gave it up (sounding too much like an oafish politician).

December 27 Picked up the phone, and only now reflected there might be messages from yesterday – and in fact there was one. It was from Anna, who twenty-four hours ago was about to take a stroll across the heath, and wondered if I'd like to come. Too late now of course, though I called back, and found her less put out than I'd imagined. We agreed to try again today.

Posed thus with the receiver in my grip, and while I thought of it, I called Hugo, who was out. I tried his cell phone, but that was switched off. Best plan now was a return to the yellow file, but the edge had gone, and having shuffled through its papers I couldn't make a decision. Here on pile A was Robert Hailer, not strictly my brief, whose archived weekend supplement finished up facedown on my coffee table. Lower on my list was the Right Honourable Lord McGey of Merridoun, who – having Grade II listed the house where C. S. Lewis wrote his *Screwtape Letters* – wanted to know why Hugo had passed up opportunities to pay a visit. Well, it's like this, milord….

I gave the whole thing up when, at a few minutes to two, I stepped across to number 8. The sisters were in retreat, with a pot of coffee planted on the kitchen table, and a chair apiece on opposite flanks. Not all was well, I sensed. Emma was tired and drawn, and puffy round the eyes, and paler than usual. Conversely Anna had spared few pains at her vanity glass, her hair looking straighter than was natural, and her glance transformed by the laborious use of tweezers (it made actual or illusory a higher line to her eyebrows). Her thin lips were fixed and unsmiling, and there was an angry flush of pink her foundation didn't disguise. When Charlotte blundered in on this, munching a chocolate muffin, and togged in ankle boots and tartan dungarees, it did not dispel a pervasive, oppressive atmosphere. Emma pierced the gloom, fussing with her niece, who must be wrapped up warm for her walk across the heath. She produced a pullover and helped her drag it on, an operation she repeated with her fleece, which she zipped from waist to chin.

The three of us ventured out, leaving Emma unapologetic and alone. Anna brightened palpably once over the threshold, much freer away from the house and braced by the open air. Strange laughter we contrived, when not much seemed to warrant it. There was, crossing our path, a couple talkative via the dog they walked, but silent each to each, and a small gang of youths, who hurled their boomerang with deep, joyless zeal. She asked what grave affairs of state pressed on my brow, to which I related my difficulties drafting a parliamentary cross-write.

'What's a cross-write?'

I explained. In this instance it was, on Hugo's behalf, something sufficiently gnomic (and that meant not too), its purpose to satisfy both Europhobes and -philes alike that Hugo was of their stamp.

'And which is he?'

'I imagine a -phile.'

'Why not just say that?'

I said that was complicated, though didn't trust my diagnosis, which placed Hugo too deferentially *vis-à-vis* New Labour, while not having abandoned his activist friends marooned on the left, one of whom was Alan Baines – not a name that Anna knew.

'You don't need to,' I said. What *he* thought was what a lot of people thought – that Europe was stiflingly bureaucratic, and we as reluctant partners could not penetrate a political inner core hegemonic by temperament.

'You think your Hugo goes along with this?'

'I can't write that down explicitly. Wish me luck with what I can write down.'

'Alaric – good luck….'

The conversation ended there. Again we met that couple who'd earlier loomed, still at a canine leap from one another. They caught my eye as they emerged single-file from a dormant clump of shrubs, its colour dun and nondescript, and dropletted with dew, and making vivid contrast with the bright chromatics in the wool of their winter hats. Their dog – a golden retriever – lolloped from the bushes, and having watered every compass point dropped a short length of stick, mottled and laved in saliva, at Charlotte's feet, and started to bark insistently. Charlotte recoiled with infantile discomfort, and put her thumb in her mouth, and with her index finger wrapped round the tip of her nose bent her whole frangible being inward on Anna's hip.

The woman, whose headgear matched the wild purple of her nose, tried to assuage these fears – the dog was a friendly dog. 'He *likes* children – don't you, Rimbaud….' (Possibly that was Rambo. One couldn't ever tell in Camden.)

I picked up the stick and hurled it back towards the shrubs, and with almost the same movement the three of us turned, and bemused at the pale unearthly light began our walk back home. What were Anna's plans? Ah, well, until ten years ago, she'd worked in recruitment, with a small exclusive firm whose clientele lived their hellish working lives in the boardrooms of London, or flirted on the fringes out in the Home Counties – men and sometimes women always in search of bright new predations – though Anna didn't intend a return to that.

We three, fatigued in our different ways, clumped up the stairs, and found Emma, who must have seen or heard us coming, out on the landing, about to break some news. Apocalyptic waves had extinguished the lives of thousands, in the Boxing Day tsunami across the Indian Ocean. The first we'd heard of it, media-free till now.

December 28 There remains under the wattage of my bedside lamp a plate with its breakfast crumbs, and under that – because for days it followed me round – Hugo's file. Plucked out of it today was his prison correspondence with a man with a *nom de guerre*. I call him Lemuel. Hugo, as Hugo, was once also Lem's MP. Lem's brother is Samuel or Sam, while his sister-in-law is Joan. Joan and Sam left the grind of London life in September 1994, when the latter's image archive, its revenues royalty-free and run on one-off fees, they could operate from anywhere. That anywhere they chose was a granite intrusion combed with wind and damp with mist, under a violet knuckle of rock, westward in Pentrarth, a hamlet-ette in the moorland depths of Kernow – Kernow a land of megaliths and other stony crops. This happy remoteness was also their disadvantage, a point they understood in the following June, only weeks into the life of a first offspring (a daughter I'll call Bo).

Joan being Joan was still restricted by her L-plates, and her mother – who'd bundled a hasty suitcase onto the train – had never learned to drive, which was fair given her terrors, fully flowered in her one abortive lesson way back. That *should* have left Sam as the natural choice, whose options were a fast coupé and a sober four-wheel drive – but that was the quandary. Sam had engineered his one fleeting chance of photographic rights to artworks lodged motorways away at Shugborough Hall. His first idea was not to go, but his second lit on Lem, who'd doubtless appreciate a break, and be on hand for Joan, who couldn't be without her marts and shopping malls.

Lem arrived the day after his brother left, and was probed little about that by counsel for the defence. On the day after that, once he'd togged up in hiking boots, and a set of lightweight waterproofs, and braved the rugged luxuriance in and around Pentrarth, there were ample promptings as to the man he was. A youth worker, a member of the Outdoor Writers' Guild, and qualified to lead climbers and canoeists, his not so solid defence lingered on the good honest stoutness and healthy outlook of his character (Me? Wield a knife?). You couldn't help but think the jury must have puzzled over this. But here other things concerning Lem could not explain his precarious moment with politics, or the time he'd spent in southern terrains distributing anti-corporate literature. You could not brush that aside, asking would an able counsel really have crossed the Tamar only to talk about human rights? Of course it would not.

What it did do was bat about the court the image of a man who had written for *Rockface*, the UK's foremost climbers' magazine, and until last year had led inner-city teenagers on summer retreats into forests and fens. Lem's simple rationale was this: the deprived in society see the world in wider contractual terms, once having entered a comradeship that encounters the elements, and not the city streets.

Day three. All scraps of information borne to the lee of Hugo's file suggest that Joan was lethargic, and probably lacking her usual iron supplements. We trace a leaden tread as she stepped from her bedroom, no more her private conjugal retreat, but rather the locus of too much interrupted sleep. Her own ma reports what glories there were in the sound of the sea – soft caressing zephyrs rolling in on a roaring Atlantic tide – and a radiant sun, with its yellow kitchen glare a strain on Joan with her sleepy, drooping eyes. Grandma scoured the place for dirty laundry, and insisted she didn't mind being left with the washing machine, a good chance she thought for Lem to drive the other two the thirty miles to Razy. A reddish golden glitter brightened that town's pinnacles, in whose rotating shadows waves of holidaymakers, pressed to the streets on an annual pilgrimage from shop to medieval shop, were joined by a tired-looking Joan, who with Bo strapped to her waist and bonneted roamed the arcades. Not much can we say about her purchases, beyond a fancy box of Echinacea tea, and a special brand of sanitary towel. Nappies she also bought, and a tub of coloured vitamin pills. Lem spent time examining a newly thought-out survival kit in one of the camping shops, and having weighed that possibility stepped across the street and entered a newsagent's, where first he browsed, then with some gusto bought a yachting magazine [I'm looking at it now. It's dated June / July 1995, and has as its cover a quilt of coloured sails spread out against a Mediterranean marine].

Lem's decision it was, catastrophically, not to drive directly back to Pentrarth. Instead he forsook the long home stretch of dual carriageway, and followed a winding detour up through a flanking moorland pasture, on a trail where at strange and not predictable intervals the verge was grazed with sheep. At the summit was a church, and a village green, and a flowering chestnut tree, and a hostelry he'd read about, whose name was the Jolly Jackanapes, unusually. Lem parked up. They left the car, and crossed the threshold, where he and his sis-in-law recoiled, their venue not so quaint as the brochure they'd looked at seemed to suggest. Here were the regulation posts and beams, blacked – and a lot of old-world tables darkly stained – with hardly a gleam of natural light, the windows small and square and deeply recessed. A Gothic-looking student, with a team of four or five others grouped round him, parleyed obscenely with a fruit machine, which not very obligingly had spat out only a single coin in exchange for the dozens he'd coaxed it with.

Joan and Bo retreated to the garden, while Lem ordered drinks and a round of sandwiches. That too was regrettable, since a score or so – not all of them male – and the main phalanx ahead of the group inside, monopolised the outdoor furniture, all of it heavy wooden integrated bench-and-table-style, some skewered, some not, with coloured parasols. Lem recalled that as he teetered out with a tray, Joan was perched on the only vacant bit of seat, while those she shared it with had taken exception to this. To be precise they said some awful dismal things, before Lem intervened – tragically for him. The ensuing injuries were summarised as Exhibit 64, which the judge – Judge Penhale – ruled inadmissible as evidence. That exhibit read—

Wounds to both temples, wound to occiput. Deep gouge above right eye. Lacerations to throat below right ear. Bruising to forehead. Bruising behind left ear. Nose, broken. Abrasions to left cheek, abrasions to chin. Contusions to throat and neck, impairing speech. Deeply bruised arms, chest, stomach. Severe swelling to lower lip. Left ribcage cracked. Internal complications with right knee. Both knees bruised. Ditto legs. Deep incision left palm and index finger. Cuts to hands, wrists. Damaged teeth.

He remembered gasping for breath and stumbling to his feet, only to fall again where a wave of gravel edged the car park. Others joined in and held him down, his face pinned to the grit, while Joan, unable to do more, scampered inside, screeching at but not engaging the landlady, who refused to phone the police – so that she, Joan, did. By then Lem had foreseen the end of his life, but clutching at one last hope refused to relax his grasp, despite the searing pain, on the blade of a knife his candidate assassin had dropped inadvertently – and here was the crux of it. A negotiated peace came only on the demand that he release it, and the promise in kind that they would let him go, and nervously both parties kept to that deal. How, one couldn't say, but by some miracle he drove, with Joan's assistance, cranking through the gears, to the nearest hospital, where the gore was staunched, and where an hour after that the police arrested him – on five counts, they said, of wounding with intent. When Lem inquired what this intent had been, the answer was: 'To cause grievous bodily harm – sir.'

Exhibit 64 was not the only evidence the jury shouldn't have to consider, according to the judge. The odontologist called upon to examine the accused saw his observations also withheld—

> Two front teeth dislodged palatally, the crown in the right one loosened [that crown fell out into the bowl of gruel Lem was trying to eat a fortnight later]. After a lapse [of weeks], root exposed through gum. Left central incisor fractured, with pain and swelling to supporting gingiva. Injuries sustained consistent with trauma caused by blow to face. Tooth, irreparable. Force required to loosen crown and fracture root, in my view considerable – a punch, an elbow, a kick.

Tra-la.

What injuries his assailants suffered weren't looked at either, amounting as they did to minor scratches, a point not consistent with the prosecution case – that, crazed with indignation, Lem, a Londoner, had launched a frenzied knife attack on a group of law-abiding students (they mostly Peninsula University), out to sun themselves after the last of their exams. Nor was there any mention of one other vital piece of evidence, inscribed on the till roll the Jolly Jackanapes generated on that fateful morning, a heady catalogue.

Here's what our Goths had consumed: malts, sherries, brandies, a half bottle of Pernod (all gone), other aniseed aperitifs, and a blur of disgusting mixers (coloured pops the contaminant, Scotch the hit). There was rum (yo ho), and there were cannabinoids, detected in the blood of three at least (spliff-ends there were aplenty, littered in the grass). Other veins were not available to sample, when few of those peripheral to that lunchtime sport ever volunteered themselves. To that you'd add the police – too busy with highway surveillance – who lacked the resources in tracing down the rest. It means one can't be over-simpatico for Lem, who puttered down the hill, seeking a salve for his many excruciations, while the core of those responsible dissolved into a serenely untroubled, and perfectly sunlit countryside.

Lem remained in custody for over a year, before his case was tried. He was acquitted of three of the five offences, but convicted of two. He was also convicted via charges added later of unlawful wounding. After six more months he was sentenced to twelve years concurrent under Section 18, and five years – also concurrent – because of the retrospective charges. More depressing still was the certainty of successive Home Secretaries, who ruled solemnly that after sifting through the 'facts', no miscarriage had taken place. I am looking at a press cutting from the *Razy Independent*, whose inner pages picture a beatified Adrian Penhale, on the occasion of his graduation from the Marine Management Faculty, Peninsula University – a story Joan thought worth inclusion in Hugo's file.

Ho ho.

December 29 I attribute to the age of my mattress the delicate sense of suspension that, in latter years, has cocooned my waking dreams, *if* I remember them. I lay at odds with the alarm, in a trumped-up version of myself, and watched as a more forgiving man than I had been made his forays in a hostile world look seamless. All ended as, with ghostly tread, the remorseless hour hand had moved to half past six, the point where he and I had merged, and I took my shower. The post came shortly after, a gentle patter on the mat, and was followed by, and unexpectedly – and odd because of that – a knock at the door. It was Anna again, in peachy silks, with a nightie underneath, which was edged ornately. She was pale like her sister, and in her eyes was the sombre spark you get when tired of the day-to-day.

She'd changed her plans, and was taking Charlotte back on an afternoon train. I can't say, in the dead hour before I left for the office, that much of this was more than alluded to, but there had been a flurry of phone calls to do with the tiny house that – in a remote village somewhere – they were due to move into, or already had. It was partly to do with deliveries – some Shaker furniture, to which Anna was a convert, as much for its simplicity as sheer utility, though I think the main motivation was Charlotte, who now had second thoughts re one of her cotton dresses, bagged with other not so cast-offs, and left with a local charity shop. I couldn't see the point in telling me this, beyond casual conversation, until she asked to meet again. That forced a rethink on particular views I had come to. There was a good chance. I told her to leave her number. Her cheek touched mine as she left.

A surprise I didn't find unwelcome, on crossing the office threshold, was the ghastly rejuvenation afoot for the last remaining desk, whose new occupant had piled it high with paperwork, weighting that with an enormous bunch of keys – or actually keys, fobs, medallions – or all manner of small machines. All this happened with no more warning than the voluminous cape and matching beret, both of a muddy russet colour, draped beside Avril's cycling top, hung on that upper hook I had used each morning, and assumed was my settled claim on the coat stand. No matter. Our new colleague had a name, and that was Hayley Moore – and she I learned was Arabella's latest recruit. She looked up only briefly from her screen, with no interruption to her typing speed. In that smallest dimming of her dynamo she pressed on to whatever natural break, a paragraph or section end, while her hands amazed all over her keypad. Avril I sensed beheld all this in a mood of acquiescence, doubtless having shaken hands with this new addition to our team. Ms Moore stood up, a youngish woman short and plump, loud in a crimson one-piece – one of those neck-to-ankle heavy weaves – and with a courteous smile held out her hand, which when I shook it was warm from the work it had done.

'Pleased to meet,' I said. 'I'm Alaric.'

We three – Alaric, Avril, Hayley – kept to our separate territories for most of the morning, busy with – well, with what? All seemed unwilling to test the changed dynamic explicit in our number. Nonetheless how hugely energetic Hayley naturally seemed to be, with *both* her phones – the landline to her desk, and out from the clutter of her handbag her personal cell. I couldn't help overhear long probing disquisitions with the merry voices in her ear, in the succession of calls she made or received, without knowing – and unable to gauge the context – what myths, intrigues or fabulations had moulded her telephone smile.

At midday Avril had seen enough, and went for an early lunch. After she'd gone I had the piquancy of Hayley's makeup applicators, and an all-pervasive pungency of nail varnish, when with meticulous care she rouged up her claws. At that I decided on an early lunch myself. Unusually, and what was the chance (there probably *is* an explanation) I chose one of those pseudo-modish bistros decked out with potted ferns and hung with Cubist décor. In its strange yellow lighting I discovered Avril, perched on a bar stool, not yet having got to grips with the menu, and having drunk one grappa more than I think she should have. I stood in a queue three-deep at the bar, a patient witness to Avril's passing conversation with people she vaguely knew. Then as I leaned *on* the bar that role transformed itself, into the more profound exchange she had with me.

How was I getting on? Did I think I was going to like the job? I stalled at the vastness of those questions, and groped for the right words, and as usual found the full-blown philosophical reply lost to the void. I talked inanities, having learned the hard way what *couldn't* be said about work, labour, wages, what we are worth. On our daily grind had fallen the mechanical night our human shadows passed through, none of us sure if any of it meant that much (you women I believe don't think this). On more neutral turf I must have said that Hugo I found affable, hard to pin down of course, but that the days and weeks and months ahead were certain to be stimulating. That last word I have had to think about, in retrospect, with the dawning realisation that wasn't Avril, at times – well, a bit laddish? It registered later, in the way she warned against that word 'stimulating', when I saw only belatedly how she betrayed a world-weariness, and a not sophisticated one. Any sense of satisfaction I might anticipate she told me wouldn't last long, when everyone knew they were inverse laws operating in the workplace (the job you're most suited to is the one some less suited person always lands).

'You know something, Avril, I don't?'

Her look was clannish, a man's, though the coyness of her smile was the mask on a feminine treachery I had known in the past, which makes of me a misogynist of sorts.

There were rumours, she said, that someone not as trusting as I was was sharpening whetted blades – scythes, sabres, kitchen tools – and reserved an assassin's smirk for *Risposta*'s former editor. The reasoning? *Risposta* and its brand conceits, awash with English verbs, and synthetic with affectation, had made its decrees against the lowbrow in art even before the stewardship of Hugo Blythe, whose combat tool, or his pen, didn't square with his inclusiveness in public life. That, I said, was to try to bridge the social and the aesthetic, which always *are* at odds. A pragmatist like Hugo approached each role according to its vocabulary. Rationale was never what mattered, only the perception – and so far as that went, according to Avril, in certain quarters Hugo wasn't 'one of us'. I didn't ask what quarters she meant (however much I wanted to know), but did think to ask her whom she meant by 'us', and braced myself for the usual. We the English – or those ruling over us – insisted on two absolutes: continuing class divisions and the order of social rank.

She ordered a mug of soup and a single slice of buttered wholemeal bread, and had sense enough to talk of something else. She was grouchy – 'Please try to forgive' – but since that computer crash she'd not recovered her most important data. There had been more and longer intervals between backups, and there was a lot she couldn't find. In some cases a month's work had been lost, bar one or two printouts, which she hadn't the patience to scan to disc.

'Oh,' I said.

Her lunch arrived, her soup an alphabet soup (her potential to dredge expletives). And there she was, forlorn, a bony unbeautiful girl, warming her hands on the glaze of her mug.

Someone from IT had given her belated advice as to how to protect her digital interests, a long rigmarole she thought to pass on to me, but not a good performance, as that turned out, though it served as a warning. It reminded me of events on one of those distant campuses I had worked on, long before my Benbrook time. 'What was significant,' I told Avril, 'was what is now rare, student revolt,' and added, provocatively, that the form it took was of a frustrated proletariat, pressing for a say in the running of temple affairs – by which I meant the admin block. A spokesman, his capacity to listen impaired by the headphones clamped to his ears, was self-selecting nonetheless, probably by his wardrobe. 'Born in chains' was the legend on his tee shirt, its letters encircling the silhouette of someone destined for a desk job. Added to that were party slogans coined by committee, this the best example I could just about remember: 'Got the technology, use it!' Avril took note. The argument ran so, or agitation was a better word: that the vast majority, if students had a choice, would prefer to meet their essay dates with floppy disc or email, which was just that move away from paper that to the institution meant an unacceptable loss of control.

'Did they win?' Avril asked.

No, predictably – as in any shift in power. Cited was the full range of reasons why deadlines could be missed. Network delays. Server downtime. Software incompatibility. Virus attacks. Theft even, of half a dozen workstations dotted round the library.

'Could be a useful ploy,' she said. 'You give me ideas.'

I left that seat of learning in all its negotiated chaos, happy not to share the outcome, yet at one with its student populace, ironically. I'm a man you find in every town, keen to embrace any useful new technology. I mention this only because in 2004 computers of a certain newness – such as those on our office desks – come standard with flash-drive and USB port, for solid-state devices the size of a well-used carpenter's pencil, subject as circuitry is to Moore's or Intel's law, which for decades to come ensures ever spiralling capacities. What gigabytes I have, in the eight or ten of these I keep a-jangle in my case at any given time, with a coloured dot I have coded each one with. Red is for music – booming fugues I've got; Handelian hornpipes; Haydn for headaches. These I reserve for moments late and alone at the office, with the tedious researches I know I can't escape. What other colours has my palette got? Well, there's blue, and that's for everyday data – copies of documents I'm currently working on. Therefore you see, in the binary cosmos augmented by Casteele, nothing goes astray (I thought).

I offered to demonstrate these historic liberations, but Avril was out for the rest of the afternoon, and would humour me tomorrow.

'Tomorrow it is then.'

December 30 I had been remiss, and hadn't wound my clock. Its dawn luminosity I found aberrant at ten to four, when in fact the time was nearer five past eight. The worst whenever this happens is a damp shirt all day, after a hurried shower, or the wait for an out-of-rush-hour train, with time spent gazing into blank eternities, in a station dressed in its advertising quilt. When, finally, I did arrive at the office, it had that atmosphere of an animated discourse brought to an unexpected end. Hayley smiled and typed her next 5,000 words. Avril changed the position of her chair and managed a thin 'hello'. Her mood brightened later, when having scooped my fistful of flash drives onto a square of vacant desk I told her – I showed her – how simple they were to use. At what fateful hour, after she'd trawled the internet to buy one, did I note the absence of mine I'd dotted blue? Naturally, not until it reappeared. That happened as thoughts had wandered out to lunch. I pondered at length, and remembered leaving only once for the washroom (long relief). I had found Hayley – not Avril – alone when I returned, though *she* wasn't long in coming in behind, with a warm sugared doughnut still in its paper bag.

When I got home I took that damp shirt off. I also checked the integrity of all my transit data, and found no digital imprint other than my own. What I did for the rest of the evening – for no other reason than someone had mentioned Hailer's name – was read that article I had lifted from Hugo's archive. In it I found the sectarian fire you'd more or less expect, with Hailer rendered as more a vignette, less a solid portrait. Guns went off at his expense under a loading of puns and an overall puerility. This was not its only fault, this excrescence masquerading as biography. For example, a sole showing of Hailer the student poet at pains with his trade was, and I quote, as 'café-didact', marooned and 'yet at home' in the deserts, or perhaps in the desiderata, of post-revolution metropolitan life (this is a cliché I think). One learned that his Kierkegaard flirtations had begun and ended already, having come about when nothing in our institutions raised the individual to upper mental ambits. He is accused of ceasing all public ambition with a shrilling, angry, offstage trumpet. He is disingenuous in his withdrawal from a politics mired, fragmented by its tribes. In reality this could only be his thinly veiled attack on his publisher – Exe University Press – who without warning had axed its poetry list, re-launching it only a few years later, having purged any last patriarchal voice, and rebuilt exclusively with feminists.

> Here – my cocktail of scorn –
> it's for you – a sure taste of something sour
> in the masculine succession…

From here any further premise had that faint, inauthentic patina of one minor pressure group determined to oust all others, our poet of holy dread dismissed as out of time – someone somewhat schoolboyish, whose natural intellectual habitat was continental, pre the mid-point of the century just gone. Reality was here and now, in the exciting diverse hues of that incessant calling of practically everything into question, or everything that presupposed either foundation or a structure. For myself I could not see in all these contra snipes a significant move away from that existentialism our published, and now unpublished poet, stood in the dock arraigned of. To be at odds with the cold science of 'things', with a spoken sensibility more befitting an earlier thesaurus – built from words now out of use, as if our human states of being are reductive to a fashion show – was merely an outsiderdom our own era transferred to its arts. I suspect Hailer must always stand before models made in a distant past, whose function was both political activism *and* emotional healing.

I leafed through his last EUP offering, which I had bought on Christmas Eve, a volume of fifty-odd poems entitled *Off the Party Ecliptic* (and of course that was mine and Hugo's party, such as it now was). You might amuse yourself in trying to match a poem like this (below) – one Hailer calls 'Second Coming' – with that magazine critique above, but you wouldn't have a guiding clue, in its fusion of politics and religion, as to what our poet was feeling so aggrieved about.

> The second time shall be your coming
> unto me, where I have healed the sick
> and raised the dead, and subjugated
> all realities that were ever imagined.
>
> Here, the living dance as frantically
> as in the world, where the strong
> were slaughtered, the weak exalted,
> and where the nondescript had willed it so.

These, I disallow
their penitence, and leave them only their vacuity
to contemplate.

I was cheated once before:
you made of me the Son of God. This Second
Coming is your coming unto me.

One has this uneasy suspicion that those of us disenchanted of the left, who feel compelled to write artistically about that experience, soon find in the deep recesses of our pen, or nowadays in the virtual architectures of whatever chipset has landed on our desk, a contempt for the crowd, for public opinion, and by that same paradox for public institutions. It's a curious fact that in the heat of our disenfranchisement some of us sound more at home with the right than the left. Those two polarities meet, you'd say, where the social blueprint is a handmaid of whoever is in power and a blurring of the mob, as doubtless Hailer finds to his cost.

A phone call from Hugo. His one-time constituent Lem, having on principle rejected the parole procedure, was due out on licence having served eight in his twelve-year sentence. He hadn't seen the stars in all that time (he *had* seen razor wire), and he didn't know what to do – about work, or where to live, or money – and would I like to meet him?

'Why of course I would.'

December 31 Hayley's birthday. I know this because soon after eleven she donned that ample cape and joined the queues in the local patisserie, returning twenty minutes later with a gooey mass of syrup cake, one cherry muffin each, some fine galettes, and a cream confection served on an enormous paper platter. First intimation should have been the aroma of filter coffee, the tools for which she had found in the tiny kitchen down the stairs, as she set off on her mission, which hitherto none of us had used (we were all strictly bottled water). She poured into foam cups she'd already splashed with milk, and for one distorted moment looked every inch a serving maid – that red chequered tea towel wrapped around her forearm. I did not like to say to what extent this had vandalised my programme for the next few hours or so, the green salad I'd planned, showered in fetta cubes, and soaked in balsamic vinegar, now only a distant possibility. Churlishly I thought to ask how old she was, yet thought better of it. She made clear she shared her anniversary with Sarah Miles, who was older by far – I'd think even double Hayley's thirty-something years.

Avril wished her many happy returns, and took a thin galette, politely, nibbling at it nervously. In the same extended motion she moodily abandoned her first and only cup of coffee, and left it to the whims of thermodynamics, taking just one sip when it had later reached room temperature. To my amazement, what remained of Hayley's sugar feast she put away herself, by means of little gobbets taken at intervals, on through the remainder of the morning and into the afternoon.

I could not help reflect that I must tell Hugo, the next time he asked, how my lack of rapport with the people whose office I shared didn't seem right.

No matter. By the time I *had* got my salad I'd forgotten it was New Year's Eve, and so found my eight o'clock retreat, the quiet corner in the subdued restaurant I'd entered, suddenly, loudly overrun by three generations from an accountancy firm, unleashed with a corporate credit card. After testing all capacities down in the wine cellar, their chair for the night – a man coiffed and cummerbunded – pressed me to take their photograph, and passed me not one but half a dozen cameras, once I'd agreed (astonishing where they all came from). I paid my bill and left.

Back to Linden Gardens. The pane over Emma's door had that dull green glow of light, sole issue of her open kitchen, blank to the rhythms of its microwave clock. She too must have been out, ringing in the new.

Some more of Robert Hailer's poetry, I thought, and early to bed.

January 1 This time the alarm set off on its long tinkling gambol just when I didn't want it to, and I almost got up for work. Then I overslept till nine, and did get up for work, only to run my shower and turn it off, reminded that half the world was nursing that most important of all annual hangovers.

What's going on, Al, huh?

January 4 An abrupt end to my holiday lie-ins, with the clangour of my phone wrenching me out of bed. Blear as the hour was, I did not fail to detect, though he measured out his words as calmly as the situation allowed, the beginnings of a gale. I had not suspected Hugo capable of this. He'd read this morning's press, and must have expected that I had too. This, frustratingly for him, was not the case – I was neither up and dressed, nor did I have an account with the local newsagent.

I tried to dampen him down, urging him not to cancel his diary – which seemed to be his intention – and promised to get to Kentish Town as soon as I could. When finally I arrived on his doorstep, the place was oppressive not solely with radiator heat, for here was a flushed-looking Hugo, already with his shirtsleeves rolled above the elbows. He corralled me in and sat me at the table, where the offending publication was open at the page he wanted me to read, or rather folded at the columns damaging to him. With not characteristic vigour, he jabbed an index into the tablets of newsprint, demanding to know – if only rhetorically – where its journalist had got her information from. I had that uncomfortable feeling of knowing what the answer was, the more involved the article became. Its opening gambit was a variation on an entry in my diary—

> Memos, emails – a swirl of directives generally – all from the top New Labour tent, were added to the Christmas handouts, as the party reminded itself and its members not to reveal the truth. Is it for this reason the leadership rehearses an all-inclusiveness?

I might have dismissed it as the travesty it was, but not as alarmed as I should have been – and under scrutiny of Hugo's sultry brows – I muttered something matter-of-fact, damning of all such journalese.

The article went on—

> The Right Honourable Hugo Blythe MP doesn't agree that politics is an obfuscating exercise designed to wrap a concealing mist round everything you think, for which reason you'll find him in the corridors and lobbies, in the bars and tearooms – in fact throughout the whole Westminster village – canvassing for names to help pad out his 'no' campaign, assuming we'll get an EU referendum. Perhaps

Hugo doesn't know, the French will have strangled it by then.

If not underlined by anything explicit he had said, I thought to my dismay that Hugo had summoned me to Kentish Town suspecting *I* had sourced the leak.

He demanded: 'What's it all about? I mean, confusing Alan Baines with me....'

'I've absolutely no clue.'

'What's behind it? *Who's* behind it? Why?'

Well, clearly to poke fun. I skimmed to the end, where the article concluded—

> One can't help recall our Old Labour ancients, a wizened citizenry bowed under those scholarly tomes they've lectured us from – the cold spoils of urban social life, and the rebellions. Are we now to think of our Eurosceptics not as Little Englanders – but reformers!

Well, a happy new year to you!

I tried unsuccessfully to mitigate Hugo's stoppered rage, with the placating view that nobody could read in it more than surface gossip, written by a Fleet Street hack bored with the usual jibes at the new year's honours list, in an airing tucked away on page sixteen, where it wouldn't attract attention.

'No, not publicly,' he said, but both of us knew. The Downing Street press office examined all such outpourings with a forensic eye to detail.

I promised to make discreet inquiries, without having said how clear it was my journal had been hacked, or even that I kept one.

January 5 How odd it is that a world of simulacra casts psychological shadows over that three-way floor space binding me to the other two, latitudes Ms Moore and Ms Avril Bamber are more than naturally at peace in, when surely one or other will betray her conscience. Not so, you say. Then what do I find, beneath this feigned normality – what signs do I detect? Um, well, very hard to say. Avril's looking ill, influenzal, paler skinned than yesterday. And what *about* yesterday?

Prudently I waited till she'd left, then rummaged in her waste bin, where all I found was a cargo of sodden Kleenexes, a brown apple core and Tuesday's *Guardian* – not the offending publication. I cooked up an innocent reason for behaving in so eccentric an English way, and asked Hayley if *she'd* got a paper. Surprisingly she handed me her *Daily Mail* (a foot in the enemy camp, she said), which was also not the one. Today I'm no further forward.

Thinks, Al, thinks…

January 6 …and yes, have thought. Upshot is my first task this morning was merging my private address book, which I've dumped to the blue-dotted flash drive – it's a WAB-format file – with the one that has rapidly accumulated on the office machine. The target I singled out – trojan@eventhorizon.codex, or Yan for short. I composed the following email—

Greetings, Yan, from the shady desert awnings here in the metropolis. It was you I think who warned against the labyrinths of government, and the snares I'd get myself tangled in. Thanks. Fact is my boss – same Hugo Blythe who last July came to Benbrook's summer school – wasn't looking as progressive as he might, opening his morning papers Tuesday last. Some rogue I share my office with has got her hands on one of my sensitive documents, and that – having passed through the murk and filters of Fleet Street – is reconstituted in the press (the 'serious' press), with barbed revelations re his Euro credentials. Why do I tell you this? Well, Yan, intuition tells me I'm about to be embroiled in an information war, and any edge I have on my rivals greatly helps my cause. Any ideas as to how I can intercept someone else's email? How are all my friends at Benbrook?

Best, Al

I couldn't be sure that Benbrook's merry troupe – refreshed and ready for the fray – had debarked its westward trains at the close of the Christmas vacs, for such is the working timetable down in the sylvan avenues of academe. I felt confident that Trojan would be there, absorbed in whatever his backroom pastimes were, soldering up some devious circuitry, or launching spyware at the Kremlin or Capitol Hill.

I fixed Hayley resolutely in my gaze, and decisively clicked to send. And it was gone.

January 7 A good decision. Masquerading as retro@thebarrelhouse. codify Yan or Trojan emailed the following reply—

> Good to get your news. As to your 'friends' at Benbrook –
> the 'sub-academic illiterati', as I think you used to call them
> – they're jubilant as ever, even *with* your regards, which I set
> off as a Chinese whisper, in the quads this morning, and
> later in the staff canteen. My New Year's resolution was to
> declare a republic, but you know what it's like with pseudo-
> elites. We're busy deconstructing every institution except
> our own, so nothing changes. Sorry to hear those stooges of
> Villeinage UK are giving you gyp. Send me e-address of
> proposed victim, I'll do the rest.
>
> Easy, Retro

It's possible assumptions I had made were wrong, but I couldn't deny that particular outcomes over the last few days – in Hayley's proximity, not Avril's – pointed to the first of those two names. I replied, unhesitatingly, in a shower of thanks,

> Paranoia is the natural state of *all* ministries, susceptible I
> am told to every kind of infiltration. This is the 'stooge' I'm
> after: hayleymoore@cult[redacted].gov.uk. Trust you won't
> be compromised on this.
>
> Al

That last proviso I should have known was superfluous. His next communication, abbreviated, and this time under the *nom de plume* wraith@wenlockedge.codicil, ran as follows—

> Here's a new one for your browser – dub-dub-dub dot
> viragowatch dot codec, a website courtesy me. See file

attached, and save to disc. In it is the password you will need for watching the viragos – encrypted.

Wraith

January 10 Why yes, it's here on screen, dub-dub-dub.[as above]. codec, whose front-page JPEGs are a witty conflation of fantasy steeds and a Visigothic queen, set off with sound effects – electrical twangling chimes.

Thanks, Wraith, for the password, and for everything – but how do I decrypt?

Al

The reply (from chlothar@trojan.coda)—

See file attached, arithmos.exe. The decryption algorithm, a breezy piece I knocked up over last night's beef and chips. Save it to disc, double click blah blah. The rest is clear.

Chlothar

I double clicked, and the rest *was* clear. The password is [excised]….

January 11 Am relieved this little foray into that crepuscular other world of espionage has arrived when it has, given Hugo's telephone rage. I wouldn't want eye contact, so I'm glad he isn't here. He's on assignment somewhere, at play with a roomful of blokes in the advertising industry, an outing that has happened more than once over the last few days. The thought of Hugo watching as we slither round the subject of party loyalty – it fills me with horror. I can use this little interlude to get the evidence I need, or so I hope.

Clouds part wittily, those chimes begin to sound like rain, there's a scud of hooves, and here she is, Brunhilda, opening her medieval ports on viragowatch, once I have keyed in the password. What that unveils is a drab if no less dramatic world, architectures summoned out of private texts, texts made various by plain to stylish fonts, in a splash of background shades amaranth to xanthin. And what *were* these texts? Well so far not the conspiratorial email exchange committed to the ether either by Hayley or her boss (the strident Arabella Jury, whose brief is sport and minority rights). Rather here was a plethora of unrelated matter – offers from the supermarket she did her online shopping with, spam her filters hadn't filtered, friends – a lot of them – mostly wearied by the routine of long relationships. Graced with these latter was no end of advice Aunt Agony, Middle Name Hayley, dispensed, her meditation being that men can never change. That kind of combativeness she also brought to bear on a firm called eLechtrix, from whom she'd ordered an MP3 player, which had arrived on her mail mat minus flash card. Result, a curt exchange, whose nadir saw Hayley threaten legal action via her credit card company. eLechtrix pointed out – the tone innocent and triumphal – that according to all published specifications, the memory card was not part of the package (Sincerely, Mandy, Customer Services). I had serious doubts as to Hayley as my culprit, and left her chastened withdrawal from under that final mortar well alone, which in all probability saw her order a card from someone other than eLechtrix. Tired beyond usual narrow limits, I logged myself off viragowatch, and amused myself with the speech Hugo was due to deliver to the ISBA, the 'voice' of British advertisers. The subject was obesity and how to re-educate a fast-food clientele, which in my humble view was a matter for the Secretary of State for Health, and nothing to do with Hugo.

January 12 A bad day today, in the sheer volume of useless information Hayley and her adjuncts smear unwittingly across my illicit cyberspace. Too much scrutiny of that secret e-place means I've had to work late, mostly on Hugo's speech, which I've brought home finally, to look at after dinner (dinner: a tinned sardine on a lettuce and tomato base). Not unusually for Emma, she had been held up too. I could hear, as I plodded up the last little flight of stairs, the jangle of metal objects as she searched the pockets of her coat. Then here she was, as I rose to the upper step, fumbling for her key, her face half-lit over an epaulette also half in shadow.

'It's you, Al….' She hadn't recognised the weary tread.

'Startled you, Emma.'

I had, but could I spare a moment? I said I could, and followed her inside, where with practised celerity she discarded her coat to the frame of one of her dining chairs. She turned on table lamps and curtained all windows from the howling night outside. I thought at first her news wasn't much, involving Anna, who'd undergone a minor transformation since her few days here at Christmas, having decided to return to town to look for work.

'I'm always trying to get *out* of London,' I said.

Emma *was* getting out, to a tiny settlement in the Languedoc, for how many weeks or months she didn't know. I said she was lucky. She replied it was work on a book, she as co-author, on terms the other writer's publisher had agreed – for now. 'You know what publishers are.'

'Congratulations, Emma.'

'Well thanks, Al.'

'I'll keep an eye on the place.'

That was just it. She wanted to leave her spare key, and asked me to sift her post, and in some cases open and report on, and here was her email address – emmalouette@[redacted].com. I had no objection, and scanned then pocketed the list she had written on the back of an envelope. For now the night was cold and I'd still got work to do – amateur research over the internet, which took up less time than I'd imagined (the brief: to clarify what outstanding issues determined the politically acceptable in Hugo's address to the ISBA). I wandered off to viragowatch, where the volume of duplicated emails had multiplied by gigantic coefficients, with extensions everywhere but into Hayley's workplace. Some of it I scanned, and one exchange I read in full, with her brother, in transit in a camper van from Melbourne to Cairns (well out of it, I thought). One little bit of sibling advice had as its thesis certain theoretical probabilities as to the strange, and sometimes bewildering behaviour of one parent or another. Hayley had entertained her mother, who was neither senile nor decrepit, in her small suburban house in Muswell Hill. I don't know whether there was also a father involved, though mater had had her revenge for all those years of domestic unquiet, prompted to actions she'd too often berated her children for – taps left running, lights ablaze in every chamber she'd passed through, mugs of hot tea imprinting ghostly pale outlines into the sheen of Hayley's polished table tops.

I might have read all this with that supreme indifference always reserved for family affairs, but at last I reached the conclusion –

correctly, as the days to come would show – that my quarry wasn't Hayley – for how could anyone question that hard-working girl's integrity? Reluctant as I might have been, I now knew I would have to ask Trojan to put his probes on Avril. Avril, just too self-absorbed to want to steal my diary, so I thought.

January 13 Here are just some in the cascade of aliases renewed acquaintance with Trojan dumped to my address book: einengel@trojan.derverdacht.de (when I first mentioned Avril as a potential target); whalesong@trojan.bigpond.au (when I turned that potential into an actuality, and asked for retrospective monitoring); beryl@beryllium.co.op (when the textual politics of Hayley's private life so overwhelmed that, politely, I requested that all her material be dropped). The first interesting point about this little exercise is the email – sender Tamara Sorr – that Avril took receipt of on December 30.

It was brief, and ran

> Good work, Avril. Now I think we *should* take a closer look at *Risposta* – before this latest development, not something I would have wanted you to give much time to. Discretion though….

A scan through my notes revealed, with little doubt, what that 'latest development' was, and discretion was certainly Avril's better part of valour. I say so because if she *was* now trawling through back issues of *Risposta* – that journal of the arts, politics and culture, with a doff to its Italian counterpart – she showed no sign of it here at the office. This I wondered at. I made inquiries, through the list of phone numbers I had amassed, and drew a dud. Then in a bizarre conversation with a man with a disembodied voice – owner, the tactless archivist working in the palace library – I learned I was now the third caller in a fortnight to show interest in that publication. It meant I couldn't get my hands on any copies whatsoever, unless through Hugo's archive. The problem there was should I tell him what I wanted them for? I tried him on his cell phone, anticipating I would have to leave a message, and to my astonishment got through after only one and three-quarter rings. Moreover he was dining alone in Kentish Town tonight.

I called in at a little after eight, and found his tiny dwelling filled with the smell of fried bacon. The table in his living room was littered with files. In a wooden serving bowl, having filled its first purpose, and standing in as paperweight, were the remains of a rice and avocado salad. The plate he'd eaten from was crossed with a knife and fork and spoon. Pushed out and marooned on the glaze of its outer ring was a golden strand of bacon rind. I removed my coat and hung it on a chair. He made coffee. Then it started, one of few meetings he and I ever had, memorable for qualities I *couldn't* define. He was more than usually remote, I thought, and business-like, implying without overtly saying so that Alaric Casteele was not a man he could trust. In any event, he did not refer to suspicions he might have had as to anyone other than me. That much understood, I couldn't see the job lasting into May, and began to think about my friends in academe.

We ploughed on through his files filled with paperwork, until at eleven I was ready to go. I pulled on my coat and asked casually if he'd ever published Robert Hailer in *Risposta*.

'Not that I recall.'

'He seems to think you have,' I lied. 'It's why he feels you ought to pay him more attention now.'

He remained sceptical, but I persisted, and eventually innocently cajoled him into parting with every *Risposta* he'd got, which carefully I heaped into my briefcase.

Selected articles, he said, from the early numbers – before his stint as editor – I would find on the worldwide web (pubblicazionidifacciata.com/risposta.htm).

'Thanks. I'll check that out.'

'Don't forget we're meeting Lem on Saturday.'

'I've got that in the diary.'

January 14 O these office days. Internal geography is such that mine is the desk by the door, and because my back is to that door I have to show caution – people passing in and out etc. – whenever logging in to viragowatch. Avril's is prime position. She faces out, from the inner sanctum so to speak, and so has the widest purview of our little trio. Hayley has her back to the window, and doesn't mind the draught. My best defence is always some uneventful list, compiled in one of those utility fonts – mostly an inky-blue Arial –

kept snugly under wraps with all my other toolbar populations, which with any slight turbulence is ballooned to the fullness of my screen, displacing anything that's likely to compromise or incriminate. That said there's nothing today worthy of that risk, bar the fact that my coevals – Hayley and Avril – have decided to communicate, not by phone, fax, semaphore, or even speech – but by email. It was Hayley who initiated this strangely automated comradeship—

> As you might know, Arabella is due to meet with UK Sport, and can Tamara suggest a strong women's group whose view she can represent?

Avril's response was terse—

> See list attached.

I only awaited the moment for gossip concerning me.

I sauntered home via a wine-tasting in a hotel suite I'd seen advertised on the Strand, and spent a pleasant hour making up a case or two, next-day delivery assured. I thought of Emma only afterwards, on my way home, inspired by the soft fruity reds I'd picked out from the southern Rhône. In contemplation of her expedition there, I mused she might like to share a bottle over the weekend.

Home again, and here's my chair, and here I've spent the evening with all those back issues of *Risposta*, or a sizeable selection of them. I cannot help but note the difference in tone between Hugo's contributors and Hugo's editorials. One fine example is the 1995 spring edition, whose cover photo is an aerial shot of the ancient city of Machu Picchu, its stone ruins terraced over its mountaintop, a composition splashed in the receding reds of sunset, under a long evening shadow. I cannot say there was anything drastically wrong with its articles, several on Latin America. There is though an airy fragile gossamer that separates assumed and natural authority, two strains in the same misappropriation Hugo himself feels awkward with and always strives to avoid. One has only to glance at the book reviews, where novelist X, MA, 'now widely regarded as…' etc., is simply one of those entitled acts of tribal postulation. But of course

Hugo knew – where some of those academics writing for him *didn't* – that the strictures of art aren't necessarily the strictures of politics, and the 'widely regarded' among a commercial bookish elite are not necessarily regarded at all among a core of constituency voters.

As a general formula each issue offered one, central essay, with Hugo's key responses to it accounting for most of his editor's introductory notes – or 'First Riposte', as he called that page. There was, perhaps not surprisingly, a very long reviews section, of books (fiction and non-fiction), of poetry (where Robert Hailer's *Off the Party Ecliptic* was dealt with sympathetically), of music (the whole range, from West Coast rock to Portuguese fado), of the visual arts, film, and of theatre (often the London fringe). The crosswords page gloried in large impossibilities, in both its cryptic and its general knowledge. And there was one other perennial – this apart from readers' correspondence – where in an open letter some well-chosen celebrity, known for his or her ferocious public bombardiering, was more than willing to fire off salvos some-where. I learned to skim much of this and concentrate on the *pièces de résistance*, and in one short evening had absorbed the best of its erudition in a very long list: the non-Shakespearean Elizabethan stage; the impact on our democratic process of Robe-spierre and the Terror; the decline of the English novel; Churchill's wilderness years; Wyclif and the Lollard Bible; the Chartists; the French Encyclopédists (Diderot and other *philosophes*); the English Privy Council; the Wordsworth of 'not for that hour, nor for that place' (St John's College, Cambridge); epiphenomenalism; Disraeli, Benjamin, Earl of Beaconsfield, Viscount Hughenden of Hughenden; William Godwin; another William, Hazlitt; and Babbage (and here I truncate an already swollen catalogue), with Babbage the London-born mathematician (1791–1871), inventor of the first automatic digital computer. Much had we to thank him for.

All these meanderings raised the unanswerable question, what did Avril and Tamara hope to find in Hugo's former life and work? I decided to sleep on it, and seek enlightenment tomorrow…

January 15 …not that I can say that's worked. Worse still, having bagged up a fortnight's tins and bottles, and left them outside at the collection point – a zone hatched in traffic yellow – I find every last nook inside the flat steeped in the stale odour of supermarket kipper, which is what I had for breakfast. Strategically I left two or three windows open, and set off with my briefcase for the parking bays (a bigger yellow cross-hatch), where I started up my car, a powerful saloon, and drove through the Saturday logjam to constituency HQ – a building cream with stucco and painted amber at its window frames. Hugo was still in conclave in one of the upper offices. The bar below was busy with utility staff and bedecked with a buffet lunch – a club atmosphere starchy white with table linen, and platters deep with sandwiches and chicken thighs. I took the opportunity to pour myself a tomato juice, adding lemon zest and a dash of chilli sauce.

Hugo bowled up presently, in slacks, a seersucker shirt, his tan shoes highly sheened. Almost instantaneously the room filled with party volunteers and other personnel, from *where* it was hard to imagine (lumber rooms apparently). With him were two Caucasian Americans – a husband-and-wife team – a business duo 'mightily' perturbed at the racial abuse they still routinely suffered in the aftermath of Iraq. I was introduced, Ted, Gillian—

'This is Alaric.'

'Pleased to meet.'

'As in Alaric who routed Rome?'

'The very same – my ancestor.'

'Droll, Alaric.'

The pair managed a fistful apiece of crab-paste sandwiches, while Hugo – ravenous (no kippers down in Kentish Town) – systematically filled a paper plate with the chicken bones he'd flayed. We got away after an hour or so, and took my car. It was a long drive north, our destination the depressing one-room flat that, eventually, Lem had acquired on the farther edge of Enfield.

Avril I'm sure is surprised to learn how Hugo has taken a personal interest in Lem's case, and is a good Saturday politician – here belted up beside me, engineering our course through the pages of my in-car A to Z. What is impressive, and also unnerving, is his reliance on no other paperwork (he's definitely without his document case), with a command he demonstrates of dates and times. It almost makes custom the sordid technicalities, which I was trying to grasp before our destination, that being a map reference which, as it loomed, was a narrow street lined with slabbed or concrete frontages. I have mentioned already that as a non-lifer who hadn't applied for parole –

and why should he, an innocent? – Lem had served eight of his twelve-year sentence, and had been released on licence, all of which I feel the need to reiterate. We pulled up outside the disintegrating terrace where Lem was domiciled, sole tenant in the wake of several others he had come to know by name. Most were on their own, as *he* certainly was, yet even families had transited through the warrens around him, though as I say the last of these had fled.

I could not help recoil. Decades of suburban sun had bleached the door, where Hugo, striding on ahead, bunched his fist and rapped. In his pose was that suggested aspect of apology, a mimetic action sending flakes of peeling paint in a cascade onto the doorstep. Yet nothing – no draught, no twitching nets – looked likely to stir.

'He must be out,' I said.

'Have patience, Al.'

The thing I didn't know, because Hugo hadn't said till now, was that the latter spate of prison beatings – perhaps climactic, now that the end had come – had resulted in a broken tibia. Certain complications with the hospitalisation process, or specifically the steel pin inserted in his shin, meant that Lem still had to walk with crutches.

I queried, incredulous: 'Prison beatings, Hugo?'

'So he says.'

Bad diet too, evidently. Lem, a mere spectre of that outdoor colossus who'd conquered cloudy mountaintops, or riven his canoe through foaming rapids, unlatched and opened the door with enormous deliberation, and stood leaning on his crutch, tall, bony, limpid-browed.

'Glad you could come,' he said.

'Lem, this is Alaric – or call him Al. He's going to help us with the paperwork.'

We shook hands, Lem unnaturally precarious, over-taxing his support. He led us in through a square hallway – dust, discoloured walls, a gated stair – and across the naked boards to the room he occupied, or just about so…. He'd borne, he said, the 'usual' spell of homelessness since his day of release (bright sunny morning, that), and, as he also explained, it had taken the probation service six excruciating weeks to approve even this address.

'Nice place,' I *didn't* say. For his nights ahead, and his dreams, here was his quilted sleeping bag, sprinkled out on brightly coloured roll mats. Kitchen facilities were: a two-ring electric hob, and a fridge no bigger than Emma's television set. He'd had a can of beans for lunch, whose orange residue smeared his plastic crockery. The décor – an ancient yellow plaster gummed with a few final tears of paper hard to strip away – he asked us kindly to excuse. In his present infirmity there seemed so little he could do. He was sorry too at the paucity of natural light, and got the two of us to shift the small deal table – here we spent the next hour working – directly underneath his one, central rose, bulbed but shadeless. That, Hugo, *you* can turn on.

So, friends, what was this bureaucracy that Alaric, or Al, was going to help them with? Well, for one thing, Lem had not been given access to any of his legal papers, or even his few possessions. For another, there was still no word from the Criminal Cases Review Commission.

Said Hugo: 'Here's the number, Al – and a name.'

'Why thanks. I'll press on with that first thing Monday.'

Various other minutes were generated from that meeting, all of which bore my initials, AGC – a gullible comrade – in the column marked action points.

A good host Lem turned out to be, who made us a milkless coffee each – a tarry distillation that I for one allowed to cool in the mug, and failed in my natural generosity beyond a reluctant mouthful. Hugo was much more encouraging, leaving only a volcanic residue of ash where his own allocation – a muddy fire fit for purgatorial libation – he drained unflinchingly.

After a sad half-hour of this the meeting drew to a close, with regrets that at the moment Lem didn't have a phone – landline or otherwise – and no email persona either. Therefore communication meant handwritten cards or notelets to and from his present address, a dreary evocation I committed to my pocketbook without much comment (Coldham Wash, or something like). He waved us off, to the clunk of both car doors, a lonely figure crumpled in his porch, his free hand hopeful in its valediction, the other in a skeletal grip on the grey metal of that one supporting crutch. I'm afraid Hugo chose this as the moment to jettison his mastery over my A to Z, all routes and traffic systems doomed to slippage when he attempted conversation. Touched I might have been to learn that the new Home Secretary, a man not known for too many mishaps, wouldn't want to start with tasks anew, and probably wouldn't help, especially now in the wake of a predecessor, who'd been beset by indiscretions destined for a first public airing. More spectacular than that – because I didn't read these signs for what they were (or even the country milestones) – was how assured I was in cranking down the gears. That certainty I brought to a labyrinth of cobbled one-way streets, the place some nether conurbation somewhere.

Hugo leafed from page to gridded page, thence to the index, too minuscule in the absence of his reading specs, and confessed, in sweeping a lone strand of hair backwards off his forehead, that he was clueless as to where we were.

'That isn't politically speaking, Hugo, is it?'

'Al, you have these soft acerbic ways.'

No matter. The road we purred along – incongruously – narrowed to a track, with high brick walls a sooty brown in texture soaring up on either side, each capped by a faded cornice long in need of paint. At odd unpredictable intervals these two blank façades disputed their monotony with small rectangular windows, vertically barred, their ancient frosted panes cracked or pocked with shatter marks. Some relief that. Finally the line of traffic nose-to-tail crawled to a halt, with a disgruntled fume and echo of exhaust.

'What appears to be the problem, Al?'

Al, all-wise in all situations, said he didn't know. Others felt the same, and left their cars – doors ajar, keys a-dangle, bonnets hot and bothered – and walked the narrow pavements to see what was the obstruction. The time it took and our own curiosity negated whatever better impulse either of us had in staying put. We got out and followed. A capacious, dust-coloured van was parked at a warehouse door, where an oldish, fit and wiry-looking man was unlading piecrust table tops, an awkward size and solid enough for him to deliver one at a time. Some saw this want of urgency as surly and insensitive, or plain stupid indifference, given the precarious levels of rage in those whose way he'd barred, one of whom – with an age advantage, but whose physicality was beer and barroom – launched off with combinations of threats and obscenities new to my and possibly Hugo's imagination. I didn't confer with him on that. Result was the current table top hurled in his direction, which he palmed to the ground and stepped across, the thing spinning like a saucer. The two men squared up to one another – the old and malnourished versus all those liquid calories – the former much more alert to the bargain they'd struck. Whether they might have scrapped I cannot say, but with Hugo's intervention both stood off, and the man – indignant – was allowed to complete his work.

It did not occur to me why, but Hugo – suddenly – was sheepish and subdued, and had lost his conversational mood on the revised route to Kentish Town.

January 16 A weird mystical metaphysics underpinned this morning's dreams, a Sunday entry I have changed my mind about and *do* bother with, when dreams in themselves are a rarity for me, overfed with portents when they do occur. No trace of it was barbed enough that my decaying a.m. levitations did other than reconcile to the cold and wide-awake reality of Linden Gardens, Highgate, where I live. The fact is it was just when I buttered my breakfast toast that some of its detritus floated through my skies. Somehow I'd transposed that odd incident yesterday to some other planar unreality, where, clad in Hugo's slacks, and his brightly coloured shirt, I melded Lem's disaster at the Jolly Jackanapes with the traffic turmoil we encountered yesterday. I thought I now understood Hugo's uncharacteristic inward retreat into that interior of private passing thoughts. These, I could speculate, were of a Lem much like the saloon-bar pugilist who'd found a van parked between him and his destination. Yet that was impossible. The judge had rigged the jury prejudicially against him, Lem a kind of hapless itinerant down in those Celtic wilds, who wouldn't know until too late the paternal link he'd stumbled on. Wasn't it obvious? Judge Penhale had done his worst suspecting that his son – that beaming graduate celebrated in the *Razy Independent* – was one of the assailants. I mean, that *was* it, wasn't it? Or was it all coincidence, and Hugo had set his tread on a tortuous path of justice, a byway off our accustomed battleground, yet laden with so much potential for career defeat. I expected him to call, when no call came, and as, momentarily, I sliced my toast into four little golden triangles, I shared his agony—

You *are* innocent, Lem, I mean aren't you…?

January 17 Some few rare moments of inner peace politically, in process with these other, no less deadly abstractions – a lather concurrent with my morning shave. They persuaded me, long before I'd knotted my tie, that for Hugo protection from himself was his first best chance of survival. I began to think of ways to construct that hard veneer. I regard it as a troubled aside, now, but it remained the pinpoint of my focus until the morning rush hour, whose spillages impacted on all these private thoughts (as often they do), leaving only shards and splinters of not consequential things. For example, what manner of domesticated being expends enormous mental energy conceiving all those clever headlines, specifically for us, and destined for the morning press? As my knuckle turned bloodless, in the strap I hung from, I was assailed by new examples everywhere. But there was nothing today, so far as I could see, concerning Hugo. One other little quirk that has puzzled is the size of all those tomes, vast oceans of didactic print, in the world of fiction that publishers and editors egg their authors on to write, whose very noble aim is monuments of discourse wanting to aggrandise all that is greyscale in the world we inhabit. I have never been able to understand this dungeon my fellow-commuters bear with them in bags and briefcases, who reserve for public transport – and perhaps lunch breaks too – these huge readerly undertakings. One would have thought their busy frenetic lives guarded against, and the same idea always occurs to me – why not read a short piece by someone with something to say?

Some similar monolith barred my morning's work when, having said my cheery hellos, I emptied my case of its paperwork and combed the phone list Hugo – untidily, because hurriedly for him – had pencilled in my pocketbook. I paused, a cold receiver halfway to my ear: I thought Avril looked more than usually Monday-ish, compared with Hayley rampant in her keystrokes. No matter. Must press on. I had a name at the Criminal Cases Review Commission, and tapped out what Hugo had assured me was his number, a naïve innocent exercise whose reward was a cascade of extensions to it. That bent what lonely hearing I could tolerate to the strained vectors you find with the hums, thuds and finally an audio dead end. Personnel who happened to intervene impressed only by the improbability of what they called themselves. Many I noted down, of which these are the three unlikeliest. A Ms Torrid Troy. A Sartorius Smyle. This one I asked him to spell, a Mr Apfel Pye. Eventually the plainer Martin Mixt consented to talk about the failure of Lem's appeal, and what recourse was open to him. I told him I understood that one of the most important things about the Commission was the fact of its independence, the first requirement when investigating miscarriages of justice. This he could not take issue with, though failed to see what relevance that had to Lem. I was able to point out that I had before me the 2002 annual report of the CCRC, a body that described itself as having wide-ranging investigative powers, able to commandeer pertinent materials and solicit expert advice.

'That's very true, Mr Casteele. If I may ask, what is it you want?'

Absurd allegory, I know, but I paused to reflect on the distant moorings the simple act of picking up the phone had threatened to maroon me to, and wouldn't want to cede – to an aloof, monocled Martin Mixt – potential to send me back there. I didn't bring any particular expertise, nor had I been asked to mention the existence of further materials, 'pertinent' or otherwise. I did wish to discuss, and not via his official codes and ciphers, the probability that Judge Penhale had been corrupted by personal interest *vis-à-vis* his son. I was informed bluntly that press speculation, as an issue in itself, could not affect the safety of Lem's conviction, which told me he'd anticipated what I wished to say, and in all likelihood had referred to his case notes even before we spoke.

'I omitted to mention,' I said, but it didn't change his tone, 'that I'm acting on behalf of Lemuel's constituency MP – that is, at the time of his arrest – who is now a government minister.'

'There often is parliamentary interest in these matters.'

'And are you not accountable *through* Parliament?'

The unflappable Martin Mixt agreed that this was so, and suggested, as his best recommendation, that Lem appoint a solicitor, and that he read carefully the CCRC's publication *Getting Help With Your Application.*

'Good day to you, Mr Casteele.'

I wasn't filled with too much hope.

January 18 'Summoned' is the wrong word, yet I couldn't help think, abandoned as I had been to the cold of Emma's sitting room, that the strain or pitch of her voice – perhaps it was only anxiety – wasn't natural. I detected in it textures of command.

'Come over,' she'd said, when in the past that simple imperative had been more of a 'come *on* over'.

Presumption must have been I'd amuse myself, here on her green settee, a pale Emma alone in her kitchen trying to compose herself, with a kettle that boiled too rapidly to calm her agitations. All too forward for her, but after aeons for me, she appeared – with a mug of coffee each – with not the usual confidence in her stride. I'd already discarded a clutch of weekend broadsheets, and bored by these had turned to her travel brochures, whose sun-drenched Saturnalia, whose rosy après-ski, weren't the most obvious associations you'd apply as far as Emma was concerned.

'Sit down, Emma,' I said. 'You're not yourself.'

'Electric as ever, Al,' yet even so, she didn't know how to begin.

I couldn't count myself as automatically excepted, but was it to do with the men she either knew or worked with, and the diminished poses they had got *them* or *our*selves into, in this current climate of 'correctness'? The truth was she'd booked her flight for Toulouse and was setting off on Friday. That should have been marvellous news, but the working partnership she had expected, and that prospect of a book deal (first mentioned to me on December 21, re babysitting Charlotte), wasn't as attractive now.

Her colleague behind the project, one Professor McBride, whom she'd met hardly at all, but whose reputation she knew, now looked like a man tragically ill-acquainted with his own vulnerabilities. McBride as historian saw books he had written roll off university presses with gallant regularity, presses whose imprimatur didn't extend into the stratospheric heights of commercial or corporation broadcast. I have seen this sort of thing with academics. It's one reason I refrain from writing books, as you can see. The idea of 'scripture' seems to me too tempting in its annihilation of the world in favour of the self, with its endless tablets of text, and the appropriated authority text betrays. It amounts – as Emma won't acknowledge – to no more than the verbal solemnisation of the charade a knowledge-based economy condemns us to, whose first and lasting flirtation is with the distortions of sales and commerce. McBride's voluminous CV boasted authorship of, or editorial control over, a vast catalogue of 'standard' books, parcels of information permeating the school library system in England, but not yet lining Europe's hypermarket shelves – and not ever likely to. I nodded wisely, having met an army of McBrides at a thousand lecterns countrywide, yet remained at a loss as to why this particular man – one of many – was so problematic for her, at this point in Emma's career.

The wider world, according to McBride, was run by television men (women too of course, he forgets). He hadn't, and never would succeed in striking to the core of that cabal, yet was painfully aware of its fraternity. As for myself, who'd absorbed second-hand these and other views, I'm supposed to look for a hidden phenomenon infiltrating broadcast TV information everywhere you find it. Let's for the sake of argument refer to this as the McBride plasma – a translucence awash in the ghostly margins beyond the television screen, a perimeter or liminal place where subtle powers are exercised. To that is added more moral sadness, reflected at the start of every working day, when Professor McBride confronts his bathroom glass. Mine is a shaving mirror adequate in its magnification. I speculate that his isn't, McBride having pocks and scars, an appearance not suited to the commodification uplift our plasmic television men (women too of course) subjected their human material to.

This would have mattered not at all, but for his obsessive nature and the quest McBride had set himself – his remorseless pursuit of the 'popular' mind – which, in the latter reaches of what had so far been a faultless career, had led him to meditate on a centuries-old medallion unearthed near Rennes-les-Bains. The myths, legends, histories (histories a little thin) that over the decades had accreted to this article had reached such extravagant proportions that sober analysis was urgently called for. Implicit in that task, first described on that evening I baby-sat her niece, was her assumption that her part in it was for the knowledge she had, and her expertise, McBride wanting her no-nonsense analysis brought to bear on this mystical and mystifying coin. She suspected now that this was a wrong assumption, when before she'd had no doubt she'd be doing serious science, with an outcome dependent on the quality of their research, and a conclusion to challenge the best-selling confection a first author had sold his books by, with countless others imitating.

I wasn't familiar with the literature, despite the proliferation of websites devoted to it, and numerous TV documentaries, whose first screening was as far back as the 1960s. She paused, astonished, but corrected my ignorance tenderly enough. The true cause of Christianity, she said, had been subverted, even at its inception, and that explained the persistence of Manichaean beliefs, so tenacious in their grip they still remained the virtual parallel of orthodox

Church teachings. The sect that had flourished south of Toulouse, in the twelfth and thirteenth centuries, accepted our fallen state, but like all Manichaeans preached a dual principle of good and evil, where all matter, including stars, comets, and human materiality, belonged to the latter, and only the discarnate part of things (for us our souls) was good. It was the object of good to detach itself from evil, rather than merely promote itself in a corrupt and corrupting world. Yet to join this priesthood required the purchase of a lottery medallion, a small dull coin engraved with a man's shaven head on one side, and a sprig of sea holly on the other. Enormous sums changed hands in the acquisition of this token, a convention one couldn't help view as oxymoronic, money, and stashes of it, the deadweight of evil in the wealth of earthly goods it represented, yet the only sure entry into a community of the elect, where the presence of any such impediment was systematically purged. It seemed McBride, rather than disprove that myth historically, preferred to add his reputation to its perpetuation, and was impressed by the number of book-club titles now being adapted for radio and TV, scope for which his agent had in mind when negotiating paperback rights.

I sensed her unease in the way she wrapped her knitted shawl more tightly on her shoulders, not convinced the medallion was unique – if but one only had been found. She showed her indignation, not at the research project itself, whose conclusions were already known, but at what had been the elaborate deception to draw her in at all. (How many of those had *I* been co-opted into?) She got up suddenly, automatically switching on more table lamps, Emma a marooned figure caught in their light, and with a penumbra slanting across her brows. I noted for the first time a faintness of freckles across the ridge of her nose and dotting her cheeks, perhaps visible only against this paleness of her flesh, exceptional even for her. I offered soothing words, arguing rhetorically that surely no one could bind her contractually to a book whose premise there was little supporting evidence for. *She'd* assumed that too, but was beginning to see how men in general organised their careers. She meant by it that all on my side of the House was a fabric of lies. Our conversation drew to a close – more awkward for her than for me, I think. She produced a latchkey, her only spare, and asked if I planned to be here on Wednesday the 26th. Anna had arranged job interviews and would be using her flat for three, four days.

'I could meet her off the train,' I said. 'Why not ask her to ring me....'

That was fine, and she handed me the key, explaining she'd tried but failed to extricate herself from a conference 'some way out of town', where she was due to deliver not one, but two of her recent papers.

'Oh well – if I don't see you before Friday, have a wonderful trip.'

She looked at me ruefully.

January 19 May the 5th seems a long way off, but already Hugo has begun to co-ordinate his re-election campaign. I know this because he breezed in to the office this morning, throwing off his jacket for long enough to justify sudden, unexpected entries in his diary. That document, to my chagrin, he chooses to scribe in parchment using an old monastic quill, with the result that, given the cautions and provisos where his ink has roamed, I had foresight to scan each page electronically, cradling the whole damn thing in the sanctuary of my hard drive. Hugo left for the first of his appointments – a grey coalition, poised to withhold their vote, incandescent over the council tax – though not before I mentioned those grim *touchés* I had had with the emollient Martin Mixt. Hugo pondered briefly, and despite his phone – his mobile phone – with its ring chime permanently active, his best advice was this: we should do as that sepulchral eminence had said, and hire a solicitor.

'Here – try mine,' he urged, and handed me a business card, vaunt of one of his much belettered pals, more simply known as Jonathan Swithe (that first vowel long apparently).

I pocketed that information, and with friendly injunctions asked Hayley, Avril or both to take a note of any calls I missed. 'Goodbye.'

I strolled for the Underground and meandered back to Linden Gardens. The time was approaching ten. Home, I thumbed my A to Z (Saturday's failures had taught me that lesson), and set off – thoroughly prepared, you'd think – on a solo trek for the hard cold rains of Enfield. Persistently my wiper blades skimmed a violet film of dew – two fine arcs across my windscreen – as I slewed with panache into the raw grey approach of Coldham Wash. I thought I'd found, then lost, then found his street again, and parked up half across the kerb outside his house, or rather room, with its few meagre possessions. There was every chance of finding him at home, I assumed. Late morning as it was, his curtains were drawn. In the gloom they contrasted with the same maroon in the surrounding brick, which had darkened with the rain. I trotted down the macadam drive and knocked, as Hugo had done, at the front door, prepared for the same long wait. I felt less certain as I knocked again, and knew *something* wasn't right, forced to look for other ways of getting his attention. But again, the gentle flutter of my knuckles on his windowpane ended in no reply. As I tried to peer through a crack, there was only a void.

I stumbled round to the rear of the house, into a gardened ruin, its depleted ornamentations now only the desolation after a previous age of outdoor life – with its pond of mud and slime, and choked with weeds. A linearity of low decorative walls was no longer symmetric, given the demolitions time had wrought. The back door, I found, was unlocked. I entered, into a kitchen just a shell, festooned with cobwebs, its décor and utility lost to the 1970s. I pushed on to the hall, past a back room, at which I paused in passing, hearing absolutely nothing, and was all but at Lem's threshold when a key turned in the front-door lock, followed by the door beginning to open, slowly. It wasn't Lem who stepped inside, but someone Lem's age, with flame-coloured hair, and a ruddy complexion, and in a dark shabby suit, and wearing one of those ties – this a non-matching sky-blue – whose knot size and breadth of tails dominate the entire shirt front.

'You're not the builder,' he said.

I was speaking to a Matthew Timms, assistant to the architect (Plane Horizons Ltd), who was acting for the purchaser, and had arrived – late, he thought – to oversee the first phase of 'renovation'. I choose that emphasis for one good reason. 'Late' had turned out not to be later than the builder. Prior to stage-one remodelling, due to start today, there was going to be an awful lot of dust and destruction – all the rotten plaster levered off the walls, other walls taken down.

I explained how little I had known of this. 'In fact I'm here on a visit to one of the tenants.'

All the tenants had left, he said, and if it was Lem I referred to, technically that was incorrect. Lem was a squatter – though he too had departed.

'Any idea where to?'

'Not a clue.'

Thank you, Mr Matthew Timms.

January 20 That process of exhumation begun last month, and the review of selected material – odd snippets amnestied by me, with reversals over Melissa's death toll – has got bigger in scope today. Melissa had been chortling over Robert Hailer's blog (http:// lookattheharlequins!.blogspot.com), which had amused her enough that she'd downloaded artwork Hailer had included in it. Prominent was a detail from *Telephone, 1966*, whose origin is traced via a Penguin paperback to the artist himself – a Richard Lidner – but for copyright reasons (all gone into meticulously by Hailer in his blog) it was an image he'd distorted through the digitised collision of angularity and hues. It ended in playground ambers, amaranths, bice, gamboge, gentian, and all this formed a collage rather than a phone conversation. A traditional font, in elephantine point size, adorned the top and bottom edge, and with the words 'Poet, in the grand tradition, seeks patron' announced this as Hailer's business flyer. 'What desperation!' were the words Melissa had logged, consigning it not to her recycle bin, but to the interdicting red of her filing system.

I paid a visit to Hailer's blog myself, and found disappointingly its internal links had not been renewed since a few days after Christmas. Its most recent entry did have a certain immediacy, framing itself – if loud and pert and self-conscious – in opposition to Hugo's envoy into Birmingham, when the minister dashed down there by train, in response to the public axing of one of that city's theatre productions. Said Hailer, under the crossfire of all the libertarian furore just then—

What free speech? As everyone spouting it knows, it's the controlling cognoscenti who decide who may and may not have it. We even have institutions whose sole function is to select and sort from the voices that shan't the voices that shall be heard. This is a process flirted with under that crumbling edifice erected long ago as a monument to democratic principle (laughable, yes). Yet all this illusive democracy has only ever been the stuff of ideals, and has no counterpart in practice. What is delivered can therefore never change – is always the froth of personal taste and the means to concretise it into fact. Whose froth we're treated to depends on what minority interest has made the most political gain.

A box-out blacked in simple inline straddled this and other edicts, and bore the epithet 'Assorted Keatsiana' – the counterweight to his hard astuteness, placed on the page as meekest irony. Its dream or degeneration was happy bands of working men, tools set aside at sundown, a brethren skirting the brow of a hillside called Clause Four, its ambience the shadows of evening, with a wisp of cloud portentous in its heaven, its glaze a pink to reddish fire, and underscored by this, the best of the couplets all this doggerel demanded—

> Reap and sing in Romantic vein
> fruits of my toil via hand or brain.

I knew I must phone Hugo, to let him know that Lem had temporarily disappeared. I didn't do so immediately because, to the detriment of all, I was just too determined to find, here in this silken exile loud with Melissa's laughter, and subject to the prohibitions of her filing system, the seeds of conspiracy I assumed to be rife in the minister's office. I carried on searching for evidence. That exercise always led, and me with a darkening thread, into the catacombs and other stratifications of Melissa's computer depths, no trawl through her archive disc divisions ever a straightforward descent from folder A to B to C. For example vectors A_1 to the distant galaxy A_{13} all had their own co-ordinates as part of that tour. What things did I find? Well for one thing she'd expended an awful lot of office hours in re-designing her domestic living space, a two-bed flat in south London, its aspect sunny come four in the afternoon, in the days in and around midsummer. A new kitchen had got as far as diagrams, their candy-speckled worktops manufactured out of crushed, recycled glass. Planned for her boudoir – an actuality by now, in all probability – was floor-level lighting, which cometh that bewitching hour appeared to elevate the bed in the right level of weightlessness for her nights afloat in her dreams. A lot appeared to go into the devising of holidays, whether solo from Penang to Marrakesh, or as a group in flight for a recently re-sanitised resort like Lanzarote, a place, I now learn, having a sophisticated village life and a dusting of chic new haciendas. To cap it I turned up Robert Hailer's flyer again – his poet seeking patron – metamorphosed as a full colour page in a country magazine, which Melissa must have had professionally scanned, and had preserved as a bitmap. What did she call that file? Answer: dogrobert.bmp.

January 21 It has been a fitful night – not necessarily on Emma's behalf – though I'm sure the car that called for her, at seven by the radio clock, was finally responsible for shooing off those bedtime ghouls tugging at my quilt. I plodded wearily into the twilit stillness of my living room, and drawing back the curtains glanced down into the street at a greyish-looking station wagon – two tired oblongs as an aerial view – and neatly double parked, with its purr of exhaust a steely ripple into the cold morning air. A man in soft shoes and wearing a blare of magenta checks – a logger's or a lumberjack shirt – one thin strand of hair airborne over the baldness of his pate, emerged from the porch with two sturdy travel bags. Emma followed him out, clad waifishly in one of her long knitted cardigans, a garment vented from the rump and sweeping round her ankles. Hers was lighter cargo – a large leather purse, a last orange from her fruit bowl, and a shop-bought bottle of water. The man loaded the luggage then ushered her into the passenger seat. I twitched the nets and turned my back, one flowing movement accidentally synchronised to an excess of revs that projected them off for the airport. Happy landings.

Did I now sense certain failures? I think I may honestly answer this, when even before the hob was lit, and the kettle filled, I phoned Hugo for the first of three attempts before I got to work. I made a second, no less ambiguous call from the station platform, as I waited for my train, having realised that the message I'd left on his voicemail he'd probably misconstrue. Recalling it myself, I *could* have meant I'd not found Lem at home, when the fact was the place we'd driven to was now a building site. The trio completed itself as I trudged into Uttoxeter Street, first with a lone pigeon, then the whole iridescent flock wheeling up around my head. I called again, at pains to reiterate Lem hadn't moved, but was missing. Then as I crossed into the office Hugo was phoning me. Avril, red-eyed and pink at the flares of her nostrils – she battling gamely with a head cold – passed me the receiver, her voice husky and thick with phlegm. 'Hello, Hugo. Where *are* you today?' Never mind that. This problem, he said, with Lem he was already aware of, a statement I could not help view as sinister. Worse, he'd hired a fleet of bikers to scour the West End, on the assumption Lem had been reduced to living on the street.

'I see,' I said. 'So what will you do when you find him?'

'I'll cross that bridge. Have you been in touch with Swithe?'

'Not yet.'

'You'd better get on to that.'

Swithe was pressing some dreary complicated case in a magistrate's court – in what municipality I wasn't told – and wasn't planning a return to his office until the end of next week. Nor did he subsequently dial any of the three numbers I left him on his cell phone, whose pre-recorded message, though it rambled fulsomely, told me nothing I hadn't gleaned from his calling card (his email ID; the precise rendition of Swithe and Co's website URL – its letters, dots and solidus). I emailed him. Then I checked viragowatch, and found that Avril *had* got a sense of humour, as she bemoaned, in a short exchange with Tamara, the 'heab colb' she'd got, what with a busy weekend coming up – a wedding, across the Irish Sea in Castlereagh. Back on duty, she shared summarising thoughts on the *Risposta* from the last quarter of 1992 – her reading matter of that hour – Hugo too sympathetic, she thought, with a Tory government in crisis over the ERM. But nothing yet they could use.

January 23 Emma, having eaten fish on the night before her departure, had bagged the bones and scales, and gone on to pen a hasty note – lamenting her time, all but running out – and apologetic should these hurried precautions not be enough, her regrets justified the moment I'd set foot inside her flat. I put the bag outside on the landing, and opened the kitchen window, which she'd left on its security catch, allowing stray winter gusts into every quarter of her house. Then to business, sorting her mail – a full doormat, tide of a mere two days. Here I encountered another problem. Three, instead of two piles naturally selected themselves: those I could open; those I certainly should not; and against all the rules a handful of refugees, unsure of which of these two identities was theirs. I thought for a minute or two, then abandoned the whole lot on her kitchen table, and marched that bag of fish bones outside to the bin enclosure.

No clear resolution was obvious, even late this afternoon, when on a surprise call from Hugo I put on my overcoat and strolled in the gloaming down to Kentish Town, so forgetting this and other minor obstacles. Waves of household warmth tumbled from his hall and across the cold doorstep, when – in socked feet, and baggy corduroys, and a zipped cardigan – he threw back the door.

'Ah, Alaric…!' (What crisis now, I wondered.)

He brewed an indifferent pot of tea, and on an oval platter piled to a precarious height the packs of crumpets I'd stood in the kitchen watching him flame under the grill. This fare we consumed in the stifling heat of his living room, from opposing flanks at his table under the window, the world outside passing by as dumb show – a man in only a tee shirt, another wrapped to the chin, then cars, vans, perambulators – all of it set off in ghostly choreography, beating time to the low murmurs of a string quintet at play on Hugo's hi-fi. He screwed up and applied a square of kitchen towel to the lick of butter that had gathered on his cheek. In a synthesised cheeriness I was suspicious of he recalled my working visit here on Christmas Eve, complete with Anna's bottle of Glenfiddich. In fact he produced the videotape he'd noticed I had found so enthralling, with all that scripted banality you get when two or more arts Mafiosi conspire under TV lights.

He pressed it into my hand and explained that in its latter reaches was a recording of one of last autumn's panel shows, referred to by him (another of his jokes) as *Soapbox Sentinels*, a corporation offering I rarely have the pleasure of, said panel consisting of, on this occasion, Leon Foch, Valery Blent, the barrister Xoey Roy, the feminist Thalia Jardyne, and a friend of Hugo's from the Lib Dems, the anonymous Marvin Rodd. In the chair was a plump, grey-haired man, who funnelled questions from pre-selected members in the audience. The venue was Dartmouth or Derby or Darlington.

'Sounds, well, mundane,' I said.

The point was he'd received an invitation, or so he said – I had my doubts. It was for one of next month's broadcasts. Given the savaging his friend Marvin Rodd had had at the gleeful hands of Thalia Jardyne, Hugo was loath to accept.

'Why's that? Is she invited too?'

'Exactly, Al.'

He wasn't sure how to cope with Ms Jardyne once she'd got on her soapbox, which in any public place she usually did.

'You mean you don't want to fall into the usual patriarchal traps, but at the same time don't want to concede women have won....'

'I wouldn't put it that crudely.'

'How crudely would you put it?'

My instructions were to study the recording and offer constructive views. And that was it. That was all our afternoon tea had been about.

January 24 It felt very Mondayish (it *was* very Monday). Mid-morning I went in search of a VCR, a sortie I knew would end in failure. The project took me – one sad and illuminating hour – to the depths of the lumber room, an ill-lit little chamber reached only through the kitchenette – another unsuspected cavern it had taken Hayley to discover. A thousand thank yous, Hayley. One viewed the place not so much as an archive, but as bits from others' archives that they didn't want, with a metallic depth of shelving lining every wall. Much of that shelving – its livery a regulation grey – had collapsed under the teetering loads it bore. And what *were* these loads? Disappointingly I didn't find a VCR. Some random things I did pick up included a batch of correspondence postmarked the 1980s, with content ranging from disaffected TV licensees ('…repeats, repeats, repeats: let's have something good, like *All Our Yesterdays*, or *The Newcomers*…') to the intellectually superannuated (where had all the Marghanita Laskis gone?). I dusted off a small padded envelope of later vintage, and to my astonishment found inside it Robert Hailer's *Razor Manifesto*, a pocketbook, you remember, and with it a printed letter to Hugo. It dated from early July last year, when Hailer's street address was no longer in Blythe's constituency. Its bold, typically Haileresque assertions weren't in present contexts relevant at all, except that some were underscored in offended red ink – I took these marks to be Melissa's – with a line of exclamation points inscribed in the margins. Such things she pointed up were very like this—

> You'd fail in these overarching debates on the role of media,
> if you thought you didn't need my help….

His rationale for that was poets, unlike politicians, weren't obliged to balance the opinions and interests of disparate bodies or groups in the pronouncements they wished to make. That alone, according to Melissa's confiscating hand, as it wielded that red pen, was ground for dismissal. So to the lumber room.

The book had a provocative cover, its colours an accident of harvest yellows, reds and greens. It showed *us* – the dead citizens of England – rising from our graves, in earthy attire, called to the last trumpet, our one final task to read aloud his ten-point plan for humanity. The poems were spare, and political, but not in a party sense, and that would discount him in later years when the lists were drawn up for the Nobel Prize for Agitprop. Lines like

> We know the mantra
> 'Come, let's change',
> is an audit trail
> of monetary exchange

or

> The social surgeon who excises our tumours
> supplies as bedside aftercare
> pills to keep us going as consumers

or central to his overall thesis—

> Orwell was wrong about extinguishing
> civil unrest. It's our television medi-care
> that soothes our savage breast.

It occurred to me that should I wish to share Melissa's smiles – she who'd ignored Hailer's overtures – then it might be possible to do so if I got in touch with him. I made a point of noting down relevant contact details entered on his blog, but did nothing more yet. Subdued at the wintry fluorescence lighting our office, and as ever nonplussed at the spectacle of Hayley's keyboard manias, and at last irritated at Avril's communal remoteness, I bade each colleague adieu and left for an early bus home. Washed, and freshened up, and revitalised by a spoon of refrigerated yoghurt, I stepped across the landing into number 8. There, having distributed latest mail across its three piles, I slotted Hugo's tape into the VCR, and having wound forward through its defiling artsbark stabbed at the controls – just me here sitting in the cold, a notepad in my lap, attentive to the screen.

A whirr in piano *accelerando* ushered in *Soapbox Sentinels'* blur of leading credits, shapeless lights that resolved to the beaming eyes and smiles, and exaggerated dress, of each guest introduced in turn. Note one on my pad—

> So, Mr Marvin Rodd, MP. A bad start already. That line in undertaker's attire doesn't disguise the agricultural physique. Brown, tousled, bushy, boyish hair is also incongruous, given that clipped, Powellian moustache.

Questions from the floor, restated by the chairman often several times, ranged from the plight of Her Majesty's Opposition to the inequities women still routinely suffered in the workplace. Rodd fared ill at both extremes. On that inept fraternity sharing opposition seating arrangements, he did no better than predictable clichés, buoyed by the glory of our Englishness, whose democratic principle allowed for all dissenting voices. That principle was undermined when they were faltering voices. Rodd's only flaw was in his failure to overcome his moral glee, when a politician's truth is always the veneer of liberal magnanimity. Someone in the audience thought as I did too, and hissed – or that might have been sibilant expletives (note two on my pad).

I suspect his fate on that eventful night might have been a lot different had the chairman – having ummed a bit and cast around – lit on someone else as first to answer on the imbalance in women's pay, a point that helped us hold the right image in our minds – namely, that artfully constructed career ceiling go-getter gals spent their lives shuffling bits of paper under. No misconstruction did he place on that boardroom metaphor, yet the innocent Marvin Rodd began his truncated ramble in a show of paternal understanding – for of course why shouldn't women be like men? To the initiated, sparks this let out into Thalia's tinder were just the detonation for each volcanic eruption following, so ingrained is our staple entertainment over the TV years (though I personally allowed my licence to lapse a decade ago). She seemed more elderly now, thicker in the jowls – not a rebel, but a matron.

I feel compelled in an almost novelistic sense to describe the weird get-up she came gift-wrapped in (note, Marvin Rodd, a good eye she had for media packaging), or what was visible over the bit of table the six marionettes went through their motions at. No longer the undernourished culture terrorist of her youth, a bewadded Thalia Jardyne appeared in a lightly sequinned swirl, a loose binding from waist to torso, culminating in several circuits round her crimsoned neck, thence over the shoulder very like a scarf. Its colour was subdued autumn bronze. Somewhere in its ocean waves was her microphone, and pinned to her bosom – which heaved ferociously – was a delicate silver brooch, in the shape of a feather, which caught and lost and caught the studio lights. All that, her deceptive apparel, only camouflaged the fatigueless metal of combat, which began on a personal note – easy to single out the buffoonish Marvin Rodd MP as the reason women *shouldn't ever* be like men. She recalled a Stone Age history of slavery and oppression (of women), and moved us seamlessly into the barbs of modern debate, where – all take note – fertilisation technology dispensed with the need for males at all. It was only perhaps supplemental that many looked forward to the wholesale gender erasure the coming cyborg civilisation promised to deliver. Body piercing was only the start.

Alack-a-day, I didn't watch the rest. These paltry notes I have made were allowed to peter out, though I mustered some few summarising pearls with Hugo in mind. Do not enter the Jardyne war zone minus battle hat and jacket, and do not try to deflect her fusillades with hopeful bluster – as I think Mr Marvin Rodd must have learned to his cost.

January 25 What revelations, watching the viragos. There exists a code of fair conduct underlying these illicit machinations in Avril's conversations with her boss. She cites instances all the time. This morning belonged to those acerbic editorials characteristic of *Risposta* in the days predating Hugo Blythe – i.e. before it decamped to neutral ground and the voluntary disavowal of munitions. What she says she can't understand is this 'disgusting impartiality' brought to every roving comment Hugo deigns to make – which wouldn't be my analysis. That said, on browsing through some of those archives accessible through pubblicazionidifacciata.com, I understand how she feels. Hugo's few if illustrious predecessors shared, it's fair to say, the same Masonic lodge, with a common vocabulary – whole lexicons in fact – let loose in a generalised artillery at any frail soul not of their social grouping.

'The best we've got,' said Avril to Tamara, 'is this Johnny Ricks thing.'

And the reply: 'In the absence of anything else, that's the one we'll run with.'

For all the attention I had paid, this exchange I still found the most enigmatic. I made a mental note to research it.

And I did so, at an unusual hour, later that evening, when – woozy under my load of useless documents – I trudged to the seat by my sitting-room window. All that extra paperwork would have to wait, as I began that trawl through all the 'First Ripostes' I'd so far managed to collect.

I got nowhere. That was because Mr Buckler, from the floor below, an old man who cared for his ailing wife in the flat beneath Emma's, knocked gently, then loudly on my door. It was late, he explained, but this was a serious situation, as I'd see if I followed him down the stairs to where he lived at number 6. I stepped inside, where his lights were ablaze, in an atmosphere a tint of blue, and abloom with the reek of fried dinner. He led me to the kitchen, he a small slight man with a mottled crown, forlorn in his carpet slippers, yet comfortably drear in a dun, baggy, jacketless suit. His shirt was the pale-green flotsam of a thousand weekly washes, as I saw from the collar, survivor of an era long behind us fashion-wise. He pointed to a yellow square of ceiling directly above the draining board, flaking uncontrollably, and swollen with moisture, and about to release the first in a bright cascade of drips. We were, of course, directly underneath *Emma's* kitchen.

'I'd ask the girl upstairs,' he said, 'but she's not there.'

'Yes, she's away. I've got a key. I'll have a little look.'

I discovered that where she had left her kitchen window open, a freak combination of wind speed and direction, and an overnight drop in temperature, had burst the pipe running floor-to-ceiling adjacent to Emma's draining board. Luckily for Mr Buckler and his wife, much of its deluge was swirling down her sink, though there was spillage soaking through the floor.

The mains tap I turned off, and mopped up as best I could. I returned to number 6, where I told Mr Buckler to get his damage repaired and send me the bill, which left him less woebegone. In fact he was mute with astonishment.

Finally I locked Emma's flat, and with her key in hand recalled I was meant to meet Anna tomorrow and hand it over. A message she'd left on my voicemail told me what time to be at Charing Cross, or failing that she would call for me at home, or if I wasn't there I'd find her in the Dartmouth Arms.

I emailed Emma, having decided not to trouble her with news of her plumbing, instead asking about that third pile of envelopes, the bulk of it doubtless advertising dressed as something hugely important. As a PS – and here was my subterfuge, here was my actual motive – I mentioned Hugo's imminent encounter with Thalia Jardyne, and asked her what, if anything, she could tell me about that TV demagogue (not the words I used of course). I was certain she was able to offer something, since two enormous tomes, and three lesser slabs, all authored by Jardyne, had shelf space with Emma's other feminists.

I was too tired for a return to *Risposta*, with that fruitless search for whatever disrespectful words Hugo, in one of his editorials, had reserved for the popular crooner Sir Johnny Ricks (a *nom de théâtre* the plainer Matthew White lit on in a previous decade). I gave up and went to bed.

January 26 Deep sorrow greyed my batch of trade directories, whose entries under P offered – in principle – high hopes for the robust plumbing fraternity the geography of Highgate was able to boast, and a wider boundary beyond. In the half hour before I left for work, sole contact with that brotherhood returned, in fighting terms, only a bleary plumber's wife, who at least broke the succession of automated messages. I can't begin to guess how many recorded my home and mobile numbers, which by eight a.m. had travelled all round London.

Office day began slowly. Avril was late, arriving after ten, wound to the bridge of her nose in her old college scarf, a garment soaked in Olbas oil. The usual dead routine brightened come the afternoon, when first one plumber, then another, then a medley, in the same laborious phone voice, showed touching concern for Emma's leak. Hayley, unused to any such remission in her keystrokes, sat with frozen hands poised inches above her keyboard, listening in. She was incredulous that, unapologetic a misogynist as patently I was, my relationship with a woman and near neighbour was cordial. I arranged for someone to call on Friday – whether morning, afternoon he couldn't say. Recklessly, I told him to pick up the key from Mr Buckler down at number 6. That old gent obligingly agreed, when later – in a fug of frying sausages – I troubled him and his wife, introducing them to Emma's sister Anna.

And what of Anna? I met her at Charing Cross, as she strolled from her train. There were changes. Her hair was lighter than its natural brunette, and had been restyled – a stiff, vigorous brush pushed up and out. And if, as I think, she had dieted, or lost weight accidentally, that had shaped an oval from the roundness of her face, and turned her geometrically into someone else. There was something angular about her limbs, with a bony sharpness to her elbows and shoulders.

Her step quickened once I'd caught her eye – just me Alaric standing there, a man with his hands in his pockets, unsure of her smile, of her promising allures, and seduced by her spontaneity. I took and shouldered her bag after we'd said hello, and led her the short walk to a low-lit restaurant on the South Bank, where we shared a bottle, and toyed with the walnut sprinkled on our salad. I managed an inconclusive hour of this, then called for the bill. That, a square of till roll folded centrally, arrived in a tiny saucer, pushed serenely to my elbow, and weighed against the slipstreams under two chocolate-coated peppermints. Both of these I left, and only now mentioned the loss of Emma's domestic water, and belated success with a plumber – a man from as far away as Perivale, whose arrival was a day too late for her. That creased her brow and wiped her smile, but all she said was oh. Oh dear.

'Never mind,' I said. 'I've aired the bed in *my* spare room.'

We taxied back to Alaric's bachelor lair. After she'd unpacked, I took her down to number 6, where we stood under the fanlight with a confused Mr Buckler, who reasoned Anna must be Emma, and couldn't comprehend my arrangements for her plumber and her key – which he agreed to nevertheless. All this time his wife was filling their ménage with smoke, and filling up the landing too, from that infernal dinner in her frying pan – whose residue stalked us up the stair and back to number 7.

At just after midnight I assumed Anna had gone to bed, though later learned that someone's TV, in the room below hers, was on, and wouldn't let her sleep. I had just arranged my bedside things – a book, paperwork, a glass of water – when with a gentle rap on my door, and in a husky voice, she announced herself. She was in her night attire, and minus makeup. She'd remembered only now to ask for an iron and ironing board, a question I had to think about. 'Follow me,' I said, and led her by the light from her bedroom door to the hall cupboard, in whose musty depths I cast around.

She set herself up in the kitchen, and draped from separate hangers a new, unattractive-looking blouse, a three-quarter-length skirt, and a short jacket – none of it that casual wear that Avril wore to work (for example). She had, she said, four interviews, one of them close enough to Uttoxeter Street I said I'd phone and meet for lunch. She expected to return to Highgate after five, in plenty of time for her train.

'Just post the key back through the door,' I said.

January 27 And in fact Anna phoned me, with garbled repetitions as to a change in her itinerary, which made so little sense I told her to meet me in the bistro. 'Tell me over lunch.' She did, in a crouch at a corner table, with her pocket notebook open. With the pen I had lent her she underscored her three remaining appointments, and feverishly changed their times – 'Before I forget.' Her first interview had overrun – had begun and ended late – so the others she'd postponed.

'You were able to do so. That has to be a good sign,' I said.

'I suppose.'

I left her at one, and didn't expect to see her again – in a sorry state – at seven when I got home. Her day had ended with a migraine. She'd run short of cash after hailing cabs and taxis everywhere she'd been, and worse had missed her train. That was not as easy to rectify as I imagined, as she'd not got an open return, and had got no money left. I almost stumped up, but thought better of it. She'd think I wanted rid of her. Instead I made her a glass of camomile tea and searched the bathroom cabinet for the tub of paracetamol I knew was there.

When feeling better she returned to her notebook. I diced a potato and sliced a leek – 'I'm making soup,' I said – and offered as one solution remaining till Saturday, when free of work I was happy to drive her home. She showered, and changed, and having thought that through spent an hour on the phone, revamping care for Charlotte, and talking to Charlotte herself (Anna only Anna in the third person: 'Mummy has to stay because….'). Then again we called at number 6, where Mr Buckler stood on his doormat in the radiant miasma of fries and battered cod. He knew *me*, evidently, and had that amused smile, and the faintest twinkle in his eye, when I'd all but confessed that here was the girl from number 8, calling for her key – a new hairdo she had or something – at home it now turned out all next day, and able to meet her plumber after all.

'That's more or less it,' I said. 'Thanks for taking the trouble. If we could have the key….'

'Here.'

'Ah, thank you, Mr Buckler. My sister would have been so grateful.'

'Sister?'

'Yes absolutely. Give my regards to your good lady wife. I hope she's feeling better.'

Don't forget to call the plumber, is what I said to myself. Then I took us both off to Emma's kitchen, where Anna, knowing where to find the security keys, closed the offending window.

January 28 Friday. Admit I'm tired of all this brooding domesticity. Result: having woken with an early alarm, I set off noiselessly, especially past Anna's door, who with any luck I managed not to rouse. Disappointingly, Avril had arrived for work before me, though not this time without letting slip important new insights into her routine, ahead as she was by only a matter of strides. I could be confident of that, because that scarf she'd taken to in recent days was still in motion, here where she'd slung it on the coat stand.

Nostalgic apparel, Avril. How *are* you today? Ah yes, 'heab colb'. [I'm watching the viragos.] But friends, enough of that. Let us try to do some work.

Or rather let us not. I am directionless, now that I can't be sure where Hugo is precisely, and don't know what he's doing. I look at the diary, which has got him in Stonehenge, talking to someone in Heritage – yet I wouldn't care to vouch for its veracity. It helped not at all when he sent this quaintly tragic email—

> Al. Looks like we're onto Lem at last, thanks to the nightriders. Have dispatched a team of three, led by Jay, and Jay it was who found him snoozing in a bin bag under the arches on the Embankment. One problem is, he's refused to say that he *is* Lem. Jay though's an excellent man, who will call for you tonight (so don't go out). More instructions anon. Hugo

Whoopee.

Or not whoopee. That is the question. (Am I going down with Avril's cold?)

Actually I'm fine. It's just that Hugo's 'anon' challenged any plain notions I had of time, which I grant are old-fashioned. I was home eating a sirloin steak, which Anna had romantically prepared – and served in the dangerous lambency of one lit candle apiece – when still I had heard nothing more. In fact it became the office tale I told her as a prelude to bed (you've got to snap out of this, Alaric), a manoeuvre postponed when a tall, sleek and leathered Jay quietly removed his helmet and knocked at the door. I didn't invite him in, but stood in the half-light of my hall, where I learned, now, anon, the instructions. These were to ride pillion with Jay and bring Lemuel in from the cold.

'I'm afraid that's impossible,' I said.

'Oh? Why?'

'No helmet, see.'

'No problem, guv.' He insisted he'd got a spare.

I made what reparations I could with Anna's cheese-and-biscuit course, then – my led treaden, and mind dulled under that mountainous repast – I followed Jay down to the street where he'd barked his pike (I think that should be pipe).

'I'm not sure about this,' I said.

'You'll be fine.'

He produced the other helmet, in colour an electric lettered red, with a dark visor. I gowned up, so to speak, and off we roared – not for the Thames initially, but the garden shed of one of Hugo's exparliamentary colleagues, who lived in Holland Park. That little construction, set back among discreetly wintered shrubs, was a favourite portal for well-known vagrants everywhere. Mostly they were ushered to distant soup runs by friendly police, or sent on their way with coinage and largesse from the retired MP himself.

'It's just worth a check,' said Jay, a man street-wise in every sense.

Check we did, and uncovered but a lone methylated tramp, whose eviction Jay didn't undertake, but saw no sign of Lem. Sedately we took in Soho, then having widened the search fell upon him, on a trawl down Villiers Street, where Lem was laying down his mattress for the night, a sodden cardboard oblong, onto which he shook out his bin bag. Again he refused to acknowledge who he was, until I removed my helmet, and smoothing down my hair stepped forward, under a bright halo of lamplight.

'We're all very concerned, Lem.'

'Don't bother....'

'But we do bother. Hugo especially.'

In fact Hugo had passed a spare house key to Jay, who now passed it to me, complete with new directives – to bus, tube or taxi Lem to Kentish Town, where having soaked him in a bath I showed him to a zed bed already set up in the living room.

I tramped home wearily, at a dreadful hour, where Anna had cleared the crockery and stoppered up the wine, and gone to bed. Aching for that bed, I reported progress, with an email to Hugo. In that same instance I emailed Robert Hailer too, to tell him I had found his *Razor Manifesto*.

A glance at a plumber's bill on my kitchen table, then perchance to dream.

January 29 I waited short eternities for the bathroom, yet once having got there and enthroned myself failed with the crossword and the sudoku, and scrutinised instead the interminable glug of foam and air and bathwater draining down the waste. I shaved, I showered, I dressed, and at nine sat down to an egg and anchovy breakfast, prepared and artistically presented by a sensationally fragrant Anna, she no doubt energised at the thought of reuniting with her daughter.

The car needed fuel, for which I refused to let her pay. 'Relax,' I said. I strode out and back across the forecourt, and saw how she'd taken that literally, slipping off her shoes, her small dainty feet snug and warm in a pair of rainbow-coloured socks. I noted too, and with disapproval, that the radio – quiet with viols and a ground bass up till then – had been retuned to a Saturday-morning glitz of casual entertainment.

Yet the journey was pleasant enough, a cascade – south towards the coast – of village greens, in a quilt of hilly Kentish fields, with leafless apple orchards in a whirr past our windscreen. We parked up and lunched at a riverside pub, and pulled up shortly after that outside the small, sophisticated townhouse where Charlotte had spent the last few days with friends. I waited in the car while Anna went inside, and watched from a distance as she re-emerged, with Charlotte very clingy. The other mother, slim and wearing slacks, and with a disrupted hairdo, held them a moment longer under the porch. She glanced across but didn't catch my eye.

Then on, where home was a timber-fronted cottage, adjoined to another like it, these two dwellings in sheltered isolation on the bend of a lane, which under a pliant young sycamore narrowed to a track. I found myself at a loose end while Anna unpacked, intent on filling her washing machine, and so took the stroll, three-quarters of a mile downhill to her village – just a church, a corner shop, an ancient inn, and a playing field. Here I paused for the match in progress, with its two diminutive teams, of just about school age – one in quartered shirts, the other hooped. Haplessly I bought a newspaper, but folded it away immediately. I started back, up that winding ascent. What augury it was I could not interpret, but above a solitary crow transited left to right, its wing-beats less and less distinct against a livid sky.

I glanced up and here was Charlotte at her bedroom window, looking out uncertainly as I stepped from the lane to the garden path. Anna was in the kitchen, towelling the floor, where under pressure of too large a load her machine had leaked. It was old, she said, and did this all the time. She asked me why not light a fire. I was glad of something to do, and set to work, in her small square living room, with spills and a bellows, and coal I couldn't ignite, though in the end, in a gathering dusk, I succeeded. We drank tea, and planned a meal. Then I shut the door on Charlotte and the TV, serving up its Saturday-night distemper. Over the washing-up she asked me if I wanted to stay, to which I replied I hadn't brought a sleeping bag.

'No,' she said, 'I mean *stay*,' and her eyes lit across to the point beneath the ceiling where the narrow flight of stairs up to her two tiny bedrooms sliced a corner off the kitchen. This I envisaged less sanguinely than she, Charlotte's bed in the room adjoining hers, and the wall between them wafer-thin. By now though we were entwined. Inclined to say yes, I found myself politely saying no – we'd have to wait – though my hands hovered on her hips, and already I'd begun un-tucking her blouse. Finally I stumbled out, and standing in the porch light fumbled for my keys. I got in the car and turned it in the lane, and drove, my lights in a blaze up and across the hedgerow. In an hour I woke from my madness, with the dark enshrouding Kentish hills starting to recede, then abruptly giving way to the grime of London's south suburbs.

January 30 Phone rang several times this morning, but I ignored it. After a lull it began again, so I disregarded it completely, in a walk to Kentish Town. Lem wasn't there. Got home and looked at my email. Here was one from Hugo, asking how *was* his charge. 'Haven't seen him today,' I said, 'but can tell you he's minus his crutch, though is still limping.'

January 31 Thrice Hayley had answered my phone, at not yet nine o'clock, leaving the same note, gummed in triplicate onto my computer screen: Hugo, Hugo, Hugo. Duly the phone rang a fourth time. The receiver when I lifted it was doused in that genderless perfume I'd detected before, if less pungent than now. I paused as the earpiece, warm from its caress with Hayley's hair, was a glowing magma once Hugo had unburdened himself. Unusually he ranted, while Avril, I noted, smirked. When eventually his fury stilled, I didn't hide my disgust, pointing out I wasn't here as keeper for the fallen, among present or former constituents. Apart from that, if he'd wanted me to spend the weekend with Lem in Kentish Town, he needed to say so explicitly. Now Hayley smirked – which Hugo of course couldn't know. Here only was the chance intersection of contingent things, its outcome a second spark for Hugo's ammunition box. He had, he said, been phoning home repeatedly from Saturday morning till half an hour ago, and so far no one had answered. I took this all in, with its spate of obscenities – all so unlike the liberal-minded Hugo – and observed in remote, officious terms how this did not necessarily mean Lem was no longer there, though I suspected that was so. That proved too much for Hugo, whose refuge was a show of parental forbearance, meting out in weary syllables a revised set of instructions. Would I please return to Kentish Town and meet John Stiles, who was already on his way.

'Who, Hugo, is John Stiles?'

'For goodness' sake, Alaric, pull yourself together! You were introduced to him on Christmas Eve.' He slammed down the phone.

I browsed back over entries above and was depressed when under that date I came across this [unexpurgated]—

> I got there as Hugo was ushering out through his hallway a forlorn-looking, wiry-haired youth – no more than. After mechanical introductions I was left to myself, alone in the tiny living room, with its tasteless décor – walls a wash of maroon, each with a spreading fan of pearls, their source a set of uplighters, opaque and oyster-shell in shape.

He was a lot less forlorn-looking when I met him today, John Stiles another of Hugo's key-holders. Under the load and gravitas that gave him, he showed me to the living room, where the zed bed Lem had slept on – probably only once – still centred the floor. Its discarded linen remained in a mountainous confection round it. Stiles turned to me gloomily, musing to himself on what it could have been that had driven Lem away. In that moment of suspension I regarded him coldly, Stiles inanimate and waiting for an answer, a man in a shabby suit, a frayed shirt, a tatty woollen tie. A nasty lurid shaving rash had spread from under his chin to the jagged contour where his collar abraded his neck.

'Problem is,' I said, 'Hugo's running round on his re-election campaign.'

'Meaning?'

'No wonder Lem feels abandoned. *I* feel abandoned.'

'You surely can't compare….'

'No. Forget that.'

A brief if sudden flush of yellow lit the table under the window, in whose soil the winter sun sowed its coin, and as swiftly retreated into the clouds, those clouds ponderous on our rooftops, and busily re-stitching an unexpected tear. Among the wreck of things on Hugo's table top – an empty spectacles case, a wizened apple in the fruit bowl – were folds of paperwork intended for Lem, which as I read them left me unsurprised that he'd gone. Someone's pet project for the homeless listed a place called Edge Connext, in a street off Covent Garden, where interior specialist Crispin Beddow had brought his expertise to bear, a man whose usual materials were polished chrome, or soft laminates, or stylish continental furniture, or tinted Perspex, or parquet floors stained every grade of amber.

'Ah, well done, you've got it,' said Stiles. 'That's where he'll be.'

I smiled, but I very much doubted it.

February 1 Stiles spent a fruitless hour on the pavements in and around Covent Garden, having spoken on the phone to staff at Edge Connext, who said they weren't sure if Lem had used their facilities, then having looked closely at his description were certain he hadn't. Hugo was furious, and on his train back to London spilt his morning tea, and had to change his suit. I personally succeeded in keeping wrapped up warm, and was severe with my earmuffs. I just would not hear of Hugo's second blueprint for biker envoys into the back streets round the West End. Stiles pleaded, but eventually I said to him, 'Look, you do it.'

I feigned meetings and other distractions, and returned home – my briefcase heavy with paperwork – shortly after two. On the stairs outside the Bucklers' was a pointed trowel and plasterer's hawk. News across the ether came from Emma, who in a long thoughtful email showed she was having as dull a time as I had had. She gave good advice as to that distribution of daily post – my three as opposed to her two piles – and explained new parameters she'd like applied to what was still to come. She mentioned the society of palaeoanthropologists she paid an annual subscription to – its logo a fossilised jawbone – an organisation that drew its direct debit at about this time of year. I must look out for a large rectangular envelope, its colour a pale daffodil – a packaging changeless over the years – and let her know forthwith how much she could expect to budget for, that part not unchanging.

These were testing times in the pay of Professor McBride, whose extramural discipline was a nightly assault on the local restaurant, its well-stocked cellar, and an excellent line in shellfish, a devotion Emma co-operated in as infrequently as the politics allowed. For much of it she confined herself to her hotel room. There, finding more time to herself than anyone might have planned for, she'd already read the three sizeable paperbacks she'd packed with her underwear. And yet, here was a useful outcome for me. Mindful of my interest, or rather Hugo's, in Thalia Jardyne, that author's *Whole Truth* she'd driven to Toulouse for, which despite its edition in translation occupied shelf space, in the bookshop Emma visited, with Hélène Cixous and Simone de Beauvoir.

I didn't begin to frame my reply until after dinner, but saw that interrupted when Mr Buckler – who now insisted I call him Alf – hand-delivered the bill for repairing his kitchen ceiling, a document he'd neatly gummed in a small white envelope, but gave me no opportunity to open. As I had so kindly offered to pay, it seemed proper that I inspect and approve his works, which he expected me to do this instant. I thought I'd tell Alf, but dismissed as just too complicated (given that confusion over the key), that in due course it was Emma who'd pay. I was also unable to say I had not wished to trouble her while she was away, working. No matter. Alf took me down, where we paused in the living room. His wife had a redundant dinner tray perched on her lap, and was watching TV, its sound muted, its screen a revolving series of pages listing winners, odds and pay-out prices from the day's races. Their marriage, he said, had seen a long, happy association with the turf.

'I'll come to you for tips.'

He smiled and led me through to the kitchen, and stared up at the new plaster, a pink rectangle, a contrast to the jaundiced white that the rest of the ceiling had faded to. It meant the overall repair wasn't yet complete, and that was probably responsible for the desolate look he now mostly wore. With steely determination, a cold blue eye – with a menacing electricity I hadn't seen in him before – he told me to anticipate a second bill, for the cost of redecoration.

'Well, yes, just let me know,' I said. He suddenly relaxed and offered me a cup of tea. But there I made my excuses, and left.

I rounded off my reply to Emma, reflecting, once I'd sent it, that had Alf Buckler not disrupted my train of thought, my pitch might have been a good deal less sympathetic. For example a tactful afterthought ran so—

No need, Emma, to read *The Whole Truth* in French. I can post you yours next door, or acquire the paperback if you don't want it bashed in the mail.

How was I to know she'd bought not only the Jardyne, but the de Beauvoir and Cixous too, and relished the challenge, brushing up her French....

February 2 Emails, emails. On the whole the one from Hugo was neutral in tone, even flirting in its latter paragraphs with definite cordialities – only because by then it had made its invitation, or issued its command. I was required, 'from six-thirty on', at the Miranda Fullbrook Gallery, a house situated in a mews off the Tottenham Court Road, an enclave sharing real estate with a New Age publisher and an Indonesian eatery. The occasion, oddly, was the launch of this coming quarter's *Risposta*, whose editor was one of Hugo's old Oxford cronies – a not very visible MP, whose bench was on the Tory left. The other important email was from Avril to Tamara, which I eavesdropped via viragowatch. All that said was this—

Look out for the table-top story – due any day now.

The combination of the two had one lucky outcome, bludgeoned as I was into sustained researches (and not that guardedly), as attention shifted back to that stack of 'First Ripostes'. Each one penned by Hugo Blythe I read in full. There was one only that mentioned – and mentioned innocuously – the crooner Johnny Ricks. In what context? Well, my friends, it's like this. One of Hugo's excursions into sport had taken him, one summer circa the early '90s, to Barons Court, but he'd chosen a day when rain suspended play. Johnny Ricks, who knocked a ball or two himself, on his days off tour and out of the studio had developed an all-round net game – and was also here in the rain. For hours the only TV spectacle was a sodden crowd wrapped in plastic sheets, huddled under a deluge sluicing off a multitude of black umbrellas. A resourceful Ricks whistled-in an alternative brand of entertainment, treating all to a solo rendition of his most mediocre hits, dating to the 1950s.

Unknown to him, there was an aside in one of Hugo's editorials: 'Forty years in the business and still the man can't sing', and that was Tamara's clinching evidence as to the elitism of the Hugo Blythe aesthetic (he would have preferred Kiri Te Kanawa, but didn't know if she liked tennis).

It all seemed too long ago to damage Hugo now, except of course that Ricks's large doses of anodyne continued to endure, and the man himself had been installed as a knight of the empire. One further complication was his many exotic villas scattered round the globe's most vivid climes, which the PM and immediate kin had access to come holiday time.

These and other considerations lengthened my stride as I crossed the threshold into the Fullbrook gallery, whose front house was lit with ceiling spots, and had a guest list that – even on a superficial glance – had settled itself into close-knit groups round the hangings and installations. Miranda, a young sixty, whose photograph I knew, smiled at me fulsomely, yet pre-empted conversation, first with explicit instructions for one of her minions, who took my coat, then with the two glasses of wine she poured, the second destined for a man with a notebook and digital camera, who having followed me in announced himself in volumes.

Hugo's Tory friend was Anton Mitchener, the current editor of *Risposta*, and member for Plaxted West. The two had placed themselves on opposing sides of a pedestal, a fluted alabastrine construct, its crowning adornment a Babel of picture postcards, these in a random upward interlock made possible through a series of incisions. Mitchener, I noted at once, didn't typify his party, despite his hair – which was closely cropped and a yellowy blond – dressed as he was in a shabbier suit than Hugo's. Perversely he'd chosen brown when black was a better matching shoe, given the shades of grey his other raiment came in. I was introduced, and learned that Anton would deliver the opening address, with a talk listed in the programme as 'Inclusion and the Market Economy'.

'Programme, Hugo?'

'Why yes. Didn't Miranda give you one? Here, borrow mine.'

Soon Miranda and her tribes led everyone now assembled down the three steps to the central exhibition space, whose feature was a series of oils – scenes, on the face of it, of everyday domestic life, but shifted to one of those impossible registers, a barbed internalised locality where all interactions with the world were disturbing in their psychology. Mitchener paused for these, yet banished all puzzlement on reaching inside his jacket for the paper he was going to read. I watched, as with a spring in his step – the man fully recovered – he skirted Miranda's makeshift seating plan, joining her and Hugo centre front stage so to speak. Brief introductions. Then a remarkably unambitious address, reiterating what every hack and commentator was telling us at that time – i.e. how important the centre ground of politics had become – with the conclusion that under *his* office *Risposta* would jostle for its place in just that patch of ground.

We filed out back to the foyer, where the reception desk had been prepared for a parting glass of wine, and a pile of complimentaries – issue ninety-three with its latest 'First Risposte' – its cover an inferno, with a garish Shadow Chancellor, a man with horns and a roasting fork, who stoked the fires of current Tory spending plans. I picked up a copy and cast my eye perfunctorily over the contents page, and was abruptly interrupted when, my role in the Blythe-Mitchener axis wrongly, or perhaps correctly assumed, I found myself among that core of the privileged invited to the Rising Sun, a few blocks away in Windmill Street. There you savoured the air, in an interior crammed with solid woods and bar stools, and still carried on your intrigues. Mine, I learned, as Hugo waved a ten-pound note and pressed to be served, were the latest result of his natural generosity, now that he was loaning out my time for a research topic an ebullient Anton – we'll stick with first names, shall we, Al – had got for someone of my calibre.

'Oh, and what might that be?' I inquired.

Hugo explained. One of *Risposta*'s new authors had submitted a challenging article on what in headline terms was the sheer Orwellian scale in the drive for citizen surveillance in the UK today. One suspected Mitchener wasn't as at home on the centre ground as that earlier pledge had seemed to suggest. Frankly he was nervous of publishing, without, that was, someone with time and energy enough – meaning me – to track all sources and verify this little-known writer's claims.

'Good of Hugo I must say to offer me your services.'

'Well,' I explained, 'Hugo's got his motives. As with all you politicals, he's got an enemy within, but he thinks it's me. This he hopes will keep me out of mischief.'

At that indiscretion Hugo paled, but didn't contradict, and after I had stood my round of drinks I left.

February 3 Sad indeed are the emails Emma sends me at this time. Last night, having exhausted her escape routes, she sat – at an early hour – with Professor McBride at his dinner. His chosen venue was a deserted restaurant, where the kitchen staff, and especially the waiter, could not help but overhear every last sigh, which from Emma's side leaked into the conversation. What was that conversation? Well, what Emma hadn't said (till today) was this. You will remember that recently unearthed lottery medallion – that holy coin she lectured me about on January 18 (aeons ago). It appears it was no such thing. Much hinged on the principles of entry into that Manichaean sect McBride had got himself so interested in, or rather obsessed she thought was the word. That entry was dependent on a particular currency, struck (you'll recall, Al) with a man's shaven head depicted on one side, and a sprig of sea holly on the obverse. McBride calmly tucked a corner of his large linen napkin between the knot of his necktie and his Adam's apple, and set about an asparagus *hors d'oeuvre*. Emma watched as his lips and the tips of his fingers filmed with grease. He didn't know that for her the project had reached its impasse with the object *actually* uncovered, a sort of spondulicks – not the right dimensions even – whose ornamentations were a salamander rather than the shaven head, and a flame instead of sea holly. All this presented no impediment for McBride, inextricably her boss, who ushered in his stewed *lapine* with the same seamless *jouissance* with which he'd greeted *les asperges*. He pointed out the powerful symbolic associations in each of these new images, whose Old Testament invocations were surely not far removed from the ideal of Manichaean steadfastness.

So let us put that to the test. According to *The Fact File Encyclopedia of Symbols*, in the edition I have – shipped from my softback book club in the year 2000 (August to be precise. I know this because the delivery note is also its bookmark).… As I say, Middle Ages folk belief insisted on the salamander as a spirit, capable of dwelling in or enduring fire. Who knows where these myths originate. Of course, this will differ from one publication to the next, but in *The Fact File* it's an entry wedged between 'Sal' ('see Salt'), and 'Salt' itself, which has its own connections with fire. Salt in alchemy ranks in importance with sulphur and quicksilver. To Emma this was too obscure, and anyway too far removed from that mythical amphibian, even supposing it was an emblem of the righteous – the righteous the person whose peace of mind remains intact despite the worst duress. Yet you can see already how attractive this must have been to McBride, who wanted to argue *his* coin was in reality a better candidate than that of the shaven head and sea holly. Moreover, the sea holly found on Mediterranean coasts, *Eryngium maritimum*, is a glaucous, spiny-leaved perennial with grey-blue stems and leaves and a blue flower, able to withstand wind and salt spray, which to the professor all but proved the point. With what disgust Emma now regarded him, the man at this point coating a continental water biscuit in a uniquely pungent goat's cheese. In one further chain of associations, he munched away and cited the *Physiologus*, an ancient text I personally haven't read – in either its native construct or in translation. Behold, one of its forty-eight sections equates that fire-quenching trick of the salamander with Daniel 3, whose verses twenty-four and five in the King James I have read as follows—

> Then Nebuchadnezzar the king was astonied, and rose up in haste, and spake, and said unto his counsellors, Did not we cast three men bound into the midst of the fire? They answered and said unto the king, True, O king. He answered and said, Lo, I see four men loose, walking in the midst of the fire, and they have no hurt; and the form of the fourth is like the Son of God.

I had my sympathies, if only because of similar presumption on the part of *my* bosses. A phone call from Mitchener's secretary prepared the ground for the email that followed, whose attachment was the draft surveillance file, with a PDF extension. 'Thanks,' the message said, 'for agreeing to look into this.' I forwarded the whole to Hugo, with a note as follows—

> Am not aware, Hugo, that I did agree to take this on. Am I really expected to perform consultancy work for a member of the opposition?

And the reply?

Yes, Al. But it's not the opposition you'll be working for. It's *Risposta*, that publication you've been showing so much interest in.

I decided the office could do without me for three or four days.

February 4 Alf had decided on a serf from the steppes of suburbia for the job of repainting his kitchen ceiling, first made known to me by the virulence of his curses, lugging his folded ladder awkwardly up the stairwell, and again later by the address and phone details on the back doors of his van. I passed him on my way out, overcome – on stepping through the outer door – at the stench of vodka – or it might have been deodorant – permeating every square of fabric he had trodden. On my way back that same all-world critique was loud in the Bucklers' scullery, a scene of unsuccessful brushstrokes, paint pots always just out of reach, or splashes to the one wafer of carpet tile not covered by the dustsheet. I even heard an exasperated wince once I'd closed my door and begun to look at the *Risposta* article, not at all curious as to why Mitchener couldn't be sure about publishing it. It was authored – surely a pseudonym – by one Lucía Lamancha, who had called the piece 'Why They Need to Know', the 'they' being that evil collective whose doings I was implicated in. The roll embraced alarming metrics as to the number of video surveillance cameras now in operation, and was no less reassuring on the traceability of mobile phones (switched on or off), number-plate tracking, the use of radio frequency ID tags, DNA sampling and retention, telephone taps, and a long list of et ceteras. From this edifice of accusation Lamancha had built against the state – to a certain extent against corporate interest too – it was my job to authenticate the enormous catalogue of sources that followed her last full stop. That in itself was a very large task.

No wonder I cast about, looking for distractions. The first when it came was Emma's next email, a plaint that, now that she'd unburdened herself, made me consider more sympathetically the challenge she'd got, looking to free herself from the clutches of McBride. I could see that any further association was likely to taint her reputation. Wild extensions to his theory had driven him to the cold bleak hills round Rennes-les-Bains, on the trail of a secret symbology, a pattern of phenomena that, in the madness of his book deal, now linked the Holy Grail, and the blood of Christ, with his shaven sect and its sea holly. She watched as, under a booted foot, he drove first a fork, then the spade he'd also brought, into the exact spot where research had led him, looking for his Manichaean treasure trove. I speculate as to the depth he dug – a volume without fruit – and have had detailed the theory that accompanied, as a new direction for him. He'd reached the point in his complex philosophy where he might have to reject the shaven head in favour of its opposite, to satisfy what he had so far looked for in vain. Think of Samson, he said – and by association Delilah too, I suppose. Think how important a cultural sign hair is, and has been, in the ways it is worn. As useful as he found the Old Testament, it wasn't all-encompassing. In ancient Greece hair as a sacrifice had ceremonial meaning, and in the Middle Ages it signified devotion or repentance (he said). He urged on Emma – and perhaps he urges on all of us – more than a superficial glance at the common clerical tonsure. Then in the same breath but a wholly different perspective he asks how was one apt to think of convicts throughout our human epochs – and not just men, often women too – once they'd been shorn of their locks. Emma said she wasn't inclined to think of persons in that stratum, but was sure it wouldn't help his cause to associate his lost Manichaean tribe with criminal elements. And what did he expect to find when he'd dug his pit? The first of his mythic lottery medallions, or lovingly pressed locks of the hair once of adepts?

There was more – coiffures coursed with snakes, and the terrifying deities they denoted – to the point that I looked for something better in the dreary sanity of Lamancha's list of materials – books, journals, academic papers, entries in Wikipedia, not to mention other URLs – a labyrinth I had to tread, all for Hugo's ministerial career, and the little damage I may do to it at this remove…

February 5 …and yet, on a Saturday morning, the prospect of Lamancha's multiple departures into the byways of state control was also unappealing. On impulse I packed overnight things and drove south, in a stutter through the suburbs, in a certainty only as far as Knockholt Pound. I wavered on the hill-climb out of Lamberhurst. In orchard country after that, in sight of a knoll, with its naked oaks, and a circling bird of prey, etched against an unearthly patch of light, I began to have doubts. I indicated but did not turn into the lane winding up to Anna's house, but instead carried on into the village, where, paralysed with indecision, I repeated the mechanics of exactly a week ago, strolling in the park, standing on the touchline, cheering on an infants' football match, then picking up a newspaper, which with hardly a glance I folded away immediately. I started back, and this time, when I did make the turn for Anna's, I pulled up sharply and reversed back out to the highway. She and Charlotte, Charlotte in a red and orange bobble hat, were halfway down the hill, but I'm certain hadn't seen me. Foot on the gas, I drove for home.

I reviewed the half-dozen phone messages left by just the one caller – Hugo – whose most recent communiqué, set down five minutes before I'd parked the car, warned that his patience was wearing thin. Not much sense did I make of it, until I replayed the first recording – left only moments after I'd set off on that abortive trip to Anna's. Here he calmly asked me if I'd read the morning press. I hadn't, of course – and still hadn't – but did have that paper I'd acquired in Anna's corner shop. A headline on an inside page ran as follows—

Minister involved in brawl with piecrust table tops

with the three explosive paragraphs beneath it omitting to say what Hugo's actual role had been – that's to say peacemaker – during that escapade. The date was right, however – January 15.

February 6 Not the most leisurely Sunday I have had. I found myself hauled before the headmaster in his cell in Kentish Town, in his mask and cape and his overall disguise as New Labour stalwart. His sense of *laissez-faire* and liberal tolerance had absorbed just one too many brickbats. For the usual professional reasons he'd got the range of weekend papers, and so was able to guide me – as he pointed, angry and ostensive – to two other accounts of that 'incident' with the van driver. I am faintly disturbed at the colour, tone and language of print and other media reportage, and in a case like this – where I'm a participant – I have good reason to dismiss our news universe as irremediably mired. No one categorically states that Hugo rolled up his sleeves and landed a blow. Indeed, no blows were delivered by anyone – yet that is not as it seems. Here, via the bastardised poetry of tabloid journalese – puffed up exactly like its authors – an innocent, nevertheless complicit readership is allowed to image suggestions of a 'brawl' in its tiny collective mind. Personally I'd never venture beyond the remit of the bridge and crosswords page. And, if you'd like me to digress, there is a much more authentic poetry woven into the abstract language belonging to the latter. Take for example this,

> For a start I am an islander, which in the last analysis is why
> I drink at home (5),

one of seven remaining clues Hugo was still to solve in his Sunday paper of choice. But there I do digress, whether you want me to or not. Hugo emphatically did not. He forced me to read every last damning word in all these mendacious articles. I really don't care to remember too much of what was written, though I am left with the residue of two highly simplified personae: Hugo's, the thug element in the PM's ministry; and mine, the New Labour henchman, one of those eternal bystanders, who folds his arms and wears a supercilious smile. I mean I ask you!

Yet the totality was more ludicrous even than that. Hugo, in some curious injured bluster I had never known before, dismissed all this hackwork only as it focused on the portrayal of himself. He hadn't seemed to discount the possibility that, conversely, the description of me did have credibility. How should I correct these faults? It wasn't enough to plead my case, though of course the situation was extremely delicate. I wasn't about to tell him how on a daily basis I had kept these outline notes – you'd hardly say a diary at this stage – when that would mean a confession, when that would mean admitting they had somehow found their way to Tamara, through her cabal. Then, puzzlingly, her possession of this latest piece of information was no later than December 30 – long before our mission into Enfield.

'Look,' I said, 'I'll make a cup of tea. Let's sit down and talk this through.'

Hugo did sit down, but stirred the cup I poured him endlessly, without ever raising it to his lips (who knew what corpses lay strewn along my career path?). I told him categorically I had discussed the incident with no one – nor did I carry hemlock in my jacket pocket – and I urged him to scour his recollections as to anyone *he'd*

confided in. For one fleeting moment I detected embarrassment –
then a sheepish look, as perhaps he *had* told someone – but then
abruptly he changed the subject to Thalia Jardyne.

'I shall have a file prepared on her soon,' I said. With that I left. For
no good reason, other than the general distractedness I was feeling,
I put my hand to my cell phone, deep in my trouser pocket. When
I turned it on, I discovered that same deluge of voicemail that Hugo
had dumped to my landline – and, a rarity for me, a text message. It
was from Anna, who said funny thing is, Al, Charlotte swears she
saw your car reversing from our lane on Saturday – but that couldn't
be, could it?

February 7 This morning the Prime Minister publicly expressed his
unwavering support for Hugo Blythe...

February 8 ...and the *Mail* strumpeted its instant reply,
condemning the Cult Minister for those outrageously snobby
remarks (see February 2, above) apropos of the PM's good and loyal
friend, Sir Johnny Ricks. The question was asked, was Hugo fit for
the office our leader had entrusted to him?

Hugo assured me he'd always been a survivor, but that sounded
like a threat.

February 9 I see it's almost a fortnight since I emailed Robert
Hailer, for only now does he reply. He is apologetic about this, but
the tone is suspicious – dangerous to believe that changes in
Uttoxeter Street will alter the fortunes of his little pocketbook. He
explained he'd been lured by challenging commissions over recent
months, and the one he'd succumbed to had kept him out of town
these last two weeks. That was borne out by his blog, which – if only
as a calendar of events – had abandoned its political edge and
dreamed a more lyrical enclosure. All this apparently from a walled
garden somewhere remote in Wiltshire, whose broad skies and
dissolving cloud configurations had spawned the possibility of
bright new alphabets, and an order of *parole* no longer subject to
social manifestations. This of course was not the moment for
critique, but I couldn't help muse, with lines like the one that
follows, that wasn't this more the recovery of years gone by, the
person in his past ejected from the polis long ago—

My clock that runs redux between the folds of time –

uncomfortably more enduring than the sharpened sentences of combat. Talking of combat, now that I'd made contact he wanted to know if the intended recipient – Hugo – had taken possession of his *Razor Manifesto*. I explained that, and even thought he might have noticed, Hugo had had to absorb the first salvos in a press campaign against him, and that was more than enough to think about, given a May election. Unexpectedly, Hailer replied to this immediately (clock ran rapid forward through the folds of time), telling me he *had* seen something, all so thin and feeble it surely lacked the power to do any harm. But that I wasn't clear about. We'd have to wait and see.

I also learned from Hailer that his politics had begun to pall, to the point that he'd no future plans for wordy suspirations such as *Off the Party Ecliptic* or *Razor Manifesto*. The latter, he revealed, had been dashed down in the sentence breaks in other projects taking up his time, in the weeks leading to the war. The Prime Minister had prayed to God, and George the Evangel had led in his family surcoat. Yet now, the purpose of his *Manifesto* wasn't merely lost. Events he couldn't have foreseen – in the wake of broadcast scandals – had distorted it grotesquely, rendering up the possibility of Hailer as an apologist of government, a man not so out of place among a clubby elite heaping its opprobrium on the BBC. I know what he means, now that I've had the point explained. The piece is conceived as a foundational proposition, where it's not so much the media in general – and television in particular – massaging our mental precepts. The villain is the politician, who nowadays has learned the skills of public imaging and successful product rollout, a nuance I hadn't appreciated, and I imagine many other readers wouldn't either.

That was no justification when, with its post-Hutton impediments engraved (apparently) on every page, he'd still decided to publish. EUP of course was no longer a possibility, its poetry list having fallen in a coup, the coup's leader one of those academics my predecessor liked to endorse – or as Hailer himself described her, 'some old slapper loud from the shires'. Nor did other houses value his name, one of life's little rejections whose outcomes were varied, and included separation from much of his hard-earned cash. He assailed his money pig in order to pay the artisans of his trade – a cover designer, a layout specialist, a digital print firm – and produced his manifesto under his own imprint, which with characteristic aloofness he'd named and baptised Morganatic Press. He certainly had a sense of his ancient lineage and subsequent emasculation. Yet all that was now behind him, he claimed. With his removal west, and the patchwork of wintry fields filling every perspective from the window of his garret, he'd thrown off the suit of political strife – I hear the crash of armour in the depths of a dark cellar – attuning himself to everything our word universe had ensnared us in, over enormous diachronic tracts. Life is long and is insistent, and is something reconstructed (rather than lived), with its lost cities and societies, ghosts that haunt a millennial past, all of it revivified with the spells we cast, with the formulas we chant, over the handfuls of fragments travellers in the desert go on unearthing, go on dusting down. Now we had Robert Hailer, with excavations of his own, carried out according to a private etymology, not of words but objects, things read aloud from the lexicon of what is (or isn't) the world. With that as your calibration it is possible to appropriate the days, months and years of all human activity to a kind of frozen Arctic ice, core samples of which poetry and life may shape into the calendars of history and myth. He asks, what co-ordinate in space and time do I coincide with, as I bite this bitter fruit? I say this sounds like religion or mysticism – though what alternatives are there, once you've abandoned politics?

Our exchange ended after midnight, with Robert having the last word, of course – which was—

> Here before the Party faithful I renounce your human god,
> and challenge your fraternity.

I had a feeling I had come across this construction somewhere before, but by now was too tired to give it much thought. I had intrusive hours before me, following every remaining thread through Lucía Lamancha's 'Why They Need to Know', and it was time I got some sleep.

February 10 If there was accidental salvation in Hailer's chants, was there something for me, with a dictum it was useful to reflect on in the wastes of *my* occupation? Viz., that in politics the too overtly political didn't necessarily succeed. Oppressed I might have been under this monolithic surveillance study, with a meandering bibliographic trail I was expected to get my rugged country togs on for, and follow to the last little desolated information hamlet. That meant hours on the internet, which I followed, round-eyed, with a concisely structured mission to the library. There was also time before it closed for an assault on my bookshop, so the net result was a number in the hundreds debited from my credit card, and a teetering pile in my arms.

Over the whole depressing day I ate just the panino I picked up *al bar Italiano*, down on the Highgate Road, and drank too little from the bottle of *acqua naturale* bought to go with it. No relief I had with the gloom of early evening, when it was clear I would have to work all night, that pitch a dark elastic span of time set for still farther voids, later when Anna phoned – at about ten o'clock. Then my ear was drugged under the seductive aural blanket she smothered on my woes, which lasted for nearly an hour. It's puzzling to have to admit that the only precise information transmitted throughout that time was a revised date and hour for a second interview one of her prospects had offered, which now meant I could meet her for lunch on Monday, which both of us knew (and neither alluded to) was also Valentine's Day.

'I'd be delighted,' I said. 'Where?'

There was a quaint little place in Soho she remembered, famed for its Peking duck, and if it still existed she'd meet me there at one. And if it didn't? Well, we'd have to think of something else.

By midnight I had done as much work with Lamancha's 'Why They Need to Know' as I was willing to, and able, and had descended mentally into that vale of fatigue where, if sleep beckons, it doesn't engulf a last little point of light. It kindled a logging-on to viragowatch, where I found days-old emails back and forth between Avril and Tamara. First bad sign was its silly misspelt chortles, a tease in the usual shades of spite, but now we have also this final launch into the wide open plain of conspiracy. Avril is saying the priggish Alaric Casteele spends hardly any time at his desk, and can't be of much importance because (and she swears she isn't counting) his phone rings only once or twice a day. This contrasts with the hot irradiations from, for example, all of Hayley's desk machines – her computer, its printer, her telephone handset and keypad. In her reply Tamara reconstitutes a lost past tense, telling us (me in my cyber patrol making this a threesome) how she had the pleasure of a happy cocktail hour, just a few days ago with Imogen Sinclair. Imogen's paymaster was the well-known proprietor of the *Sunday Plaint*, whose combustible supplement offered colourful exposés on the life and work of persons prominent publicly. I didn't know I qualified. But anon, we'll come to that. Tamara began this merry jaunt with a soda water filled with ice, touched at its meniscus with grated orange peel, which both agreed made the whole experience chromatically that much more interesting. They graduated – and at the same pace – to a spritzer, and noted in similar unison how efficiently the chiller had cooled the Chardonnay, which wasn't necessarily the better part of that barbaric mix. Next came Chardonnay straight, with each in this formidable public pairing reaching for her purse and insisting she would pay. Don't ask me who *did* pay (and anyway I'm tired and want to go to bed).

They thought they ought not to, but nevertheless dispatched several ornamental dishes filled with bar snacks – cubed cheeses and cocktail onions skewered on wooden picks. A great deal of litter they left behind in the crock of pistachios they shelled. However, let us put that aside and get to the coup – hard to describe as a flourish – though by now Tamara must have felt equal to it. I am truly grateful for the huge coloured aura enveloping the pair, as they put away sidecars before their taxis home. One asks, did they exchange their high heels for the flat shoes it must have been wise to carry for such occasions, volume of their bags permitting? (Answer below.) Tamara confided, perhaps with a knowing wink, that certain sensitive written information had come her way, which many would agree – and some like me would not – was bound to look well published in the *Plaint*, under the plain square serifs of the Sinclair moniker. Imogen giggled, as more was revealed. She was told what this material was. Here I am wounded when, according to Tamara, these diarial notes of mine have already approached the status of pasquinade, referring as they do to a ministry in disarray. If I'd suspected she was after Hugo's job, I'm certain of it now. Anyway, pasquinade or not, the thought crosses my mind that a riper version from *my* pen, and not Imogen's, is probably the only constructive counterblast to who knows what lies, what innuendoes, this disreputable double act has warmed under their duetting brandy fumes. A deal was struck, and must have been momentous, because whoever paid the bar bill forgot to collect her change. I'm careful not to imply that they tottered out on one another's arm, but I do record as fact – as Tamara herself did – that Imogen foolishly wedged the heel of a beautifully crafted Italian shoe in the grating in the lobby. This was disastrous for one whose many *scarpe* were shipped from the farther shore of Lago di Varese. A bellboy came out running at her cries and prised free madam's butchered footwear carelessly, so that as a *paio* it and its partner were ruined. *Mi dispiace.* Nor did he redeem himself in volunteering those shiny pistoles scattered on the bar, which weren't a tip. He produced an unfolding concertina of business cards, from which he selected a taxi firm prepared to send a driver right to the door that instant, in whose throbbing car, scheming in all that midnight plush of its back seat, she already knew exactly what she'd say about me. Not that I'm given to paranoia.

February 11 It is gratifying to know that having mastered the virgin terrain of her USB port, Avril is a convert. She sees the potential. This morning she was telling Hayley how she'd got herself an iPod, astronomical in its gigabytes, and had entered it as an office expense, on the ground that radio downloads were now so prevalent they vied as the best means of keeping up with news and current affairs. This was important to her and Tamara, given our obsession with the BBC, whose moral indignation it's our job to placate. No one wants a dangerous metaphysics infecting a wider population beyond the citadels of Broadcasting House. In effect this was, where none had existed before, the seal on Avril's immurement, a wraith who from now on stuffed her sensitive lugs with the double earpiece wired to her player. This, by no means the latest cybernation, resulted in a longer elapse of time from the first shrill of Avril's phone to the moment she lifted its receiver. Then came in multitudes unbidden smirks, when from beneath her quilt of sound – a false protection, Avril – I watched as she read what quirks and other confidences crossed her PC screen. Often her upper lip curled. In a sense that was a safer haven for me, as I began to anticipate every changing movement through viragowatch.codec – that's to say good reading, bad, indifferent – and logged off only when I'd got what information I wanted. Allow me to expand on that point with Tamara, flush with Imogen's article, a Xerox of which she'd already sent by internal mail, and Avril should be receiving soon.

'I've told her I'd like your comments before it goes to press.'

'Pleasure's all mine,' was Avril's instant reply.

I spent the afternoon plotting this newest of old-fashioned ruses, unsuccessfully as things turned out, for seek as I may there was no opportunity to intercept that large orange postal jacket before it reached Avril's desk, whose content she worked with an over-exuberant pen. Nor could I forestall the next leg in that document's journey, which occurred after four, when she gummed it into a large manila envelope, and having wound on her scarf, and pulling on her coat, bade us a loud adieu (still wired, she was). I considered, vaguely, following her out, but failed even to do that, in the leaden silences under Hayley's gaze, whose powers were masculine, chthonic, and kept me moulded to my seat. Best I could do was close off this unpaid commission for *Risposta* with a summary larger in extent than Lamancha's original article, and that by several cubits.

I have this uneasy feeling.

February 12 Alf, sheepishly, not wishing to overstate the second of his bills, slipped it through my door as soon as I'd left with my shopping bag. When I unsealed it, this is what I found: a cryptic, fully capitalised journal of events, squashed in the ruled void adjacent to the figures column, at pains to re-emphasise that things had gone wrong – hence this excessive sum. I wondered at this, but felt only an overwhelming reminder to get in touch with Anna. But that was also off my scale. On a walk in the rain in the valley over the hill from their house, Charlotte had jumped in a puddle deeper than anyone might have suspected, and was trembling in their little square kitchen, in the heap of sodden garments peeled from her limbs, clutching at a towel, and waiting for the bath upstairs to fill.

That was unlike Charlotte, I said, but promised to phone again later.

February 13 I upset my finer principles today and lunched on a doner kebab, whose shavings of flesh came generously dressed in flora, all of which I sluiced down with a can of German lager. I tottered home and – these excursions into other cultures not having eased my forebodings – I also bought a *Sunday Plaint*, which I read in my window, sure that Hugo would soon be raging over the phone. Here – and I paraphrase – is what the three witches – Tamara, Avril and Imogen – had concocted, heady revelations centred on a certain 'Alan Cassell', a man not merely re-christened, but promoted to the giddy plateau of 'advisor', his boss the Right Honourable Hugo Blythe MP. Installed in only the December of 2004 (see December 20 above), his rationale in accepting the post is the easy tube ride from where he lives – that would be here in Highgate – to the office in Uttoxeter Street. All that pales with what is implied of *Hugo's* rationale, who sees in a 'self-declared' misogynist only congeniality, the minister a man who finds women's issues 'ominous'. (Still the phone doesn't ring.) With what cheery fraternity these two must have packed their pipes – both of us non-smokers by the way – when the first re-cleansing task that Alan Cassell sets himself is imposing his own brand of patriarchal order, not only conversationally, but on the computer admin system he's inherited from a predecessor (a female, who doubtless was hounded out of office).

These aren't the only grounds of Cassell's unsuitability. For someone whose job is the arts, he exhibits a morbid disgust for broadcast media (December 21). When, reluctantly, one adds to that an unhealthy contempt for the general public (December 22), whose queries and concerns about the arts are dismissed as idiotic, what we have is the artificial mannerism (a tautology there I think, gals) enlightened people have railed against for decades. Naughty Alan Cassell. Again from December 22, here are my several opportunities to 'poison the minds of the young', through my predatory pursuit of a neighbour's innocent niece. Then, Imogen asks, in the best rhetoric her trade allows (which permits of changing registers, but no encapsulating question mark), is it not ironic that while these two men are incapable of organising a means of communication between themselves, Cassell has no difficulties whatsoever in passing confidential information to his neighbours, with the proneness he has for gossip about his job (q.v. December 23).

Other offences are, one (both men): the idea of working late bound to the copious consumption of strong liquor (Christmas Eve, for goodness' sake); two, Cassell, a good factotum for Dickens's

Scrooge (Christmas Day); three, the same, his professional ineptitude in never finding time to read the daily papers (Boxing Day); four, Hugo, clearly a Europhobe, but worst of all (December 27) how easily he is duped into siding with a convicted, violent criminal. There was a five, a six, a seven, an eight-nine-ten, but already I am mentally drafting my resignation – though curiously Hugo still hasn't phoned.

February 14 I got to work early as usual, that's to say a few moments after Avril, and tried to behave as if nothing had happened, though all of us had heard – for the second time in seven days – the Prime Minister express unwavering support for Hugo Blythe, who as early as six a.m. was said to have offered his resignation. My brief missive along those lines, rehearsed *ad nauseam* over a long, sleepless night, didn't now pepper the word processor with quite the syntactical convention I had dreamed in all that insomnia. Quite the contrary in fact, as – in a final act of defiance, or perhaps you'd call it stoicism – my only issue for one last day working for Hugo Blythe was weeding out the usual clichés. Therefore be gone 'the sword of Damocles', out my 'untenable position'. And for a future littered with 'banana skins', or tropical peelings generally, I censor that too. For the time being I didn't print off and sign that document, instead plugging in one of my colour-coded flash drives. From it I produced the manuscript version of my memoir jottings to date, with the intention of editing and annotating using only an old-fashioned pen. Then of course I planned a tour of all interested publishers. The pile sat on the edge of my desk, still warm from the printer when, catastrophically, my telephone rang, and at the same moment Tamara Sorr breezed in. I didn't catch what she said – something about solidarity, and Hugo's desperate hour – and anyway addressed more to Avril and Hayley than to me. My call was from Anna, who had caught her train, and read her magazine, and was watching the Kentish countryside roll past her window, and feeling apprehensive. I turned half to the wall for a moiety of privacy, and, having assured her a second interview must in itself bode well, I told her where to meet for lunch and gently said goodbye. When I cradled the receiver Tamara had gone, and so had my manuscript. I rushed down after her, taking the steps four at a time, not sure I *could* confront or accuse her. When, breathless and rouged and beaded in sweat, I landed on the street, she and her car were nowhere.

I returned to the office and signed my resignation, but rather than place it on Hugo's desk mailed it to his Kentish Town address. Avril, impassive throughout, found refuge in her iPod, while Hayley talked on the phone and scrutinised her fingernails. I left, hours before my appointment with Anna, and having trekked anonymous side streets perched myself in the cold of an espresso bar, a cubicle filled with padded stools, tall to the window. I watched, while through that glass, in the grey shambling of its citizens, the winter metropolis noiselessly glided by. I was trying to think, but not systematically, of what to do next. I should look for another job (ah well no, not yet). Spend some time abroad, with the gîte after all always available (um, well, ditto). Revenge loomed uppermost, in every possible concretisation, and what now seemed irresistible was the monastic retreat and shady depths of Linden Gardens, where with a daily regime and labour at my desk it shouldn't take long to elaborate, or even fabricate these memoirs, and grant them life publicly, before Tamara had the chance to do the same. She could only hope I was busy with other things.

Now paradoxically I had sudden, enormous vistas of time, yet still succeeded in keeping Anna waiting, unsure what to do – me with my cell phone off, and having left the office hours ago. I found her strolling the Soho pavements where her restaurant and its decades-old accoutrements had mutated into a noodles bar.

'Sorry,' I said. 'Got held up.'

She noted nothing unusual in that, and led me to another remembered venue, which without fuss served us crayfish tails afloat in a black bean sauce – a house special apparently. I allowed her to pay, as I think was intended, and managed to overcome my gloom, feeling pleased that at least for now her drudgery of parenthood had melted away. She had interviewed well, and in relating that had a lightness, even a radiance in her being.

'And you?' she asked. 'You do look dissed doff.'

'It's nothing I can put my finger on,' I lied. 'Hate these English winters.'

I saw her to the train and waved from the platform, and maundered home, where I weighed possible strategies, and even wrote a list – all of it retaliation against Tamara Sorr. The first war zone had already been declared, bounded by the midnight inks of December 29, which meant its fateful strokes in my diary Imogen might soon be asked to go beyond. I would have to revisit everything myself, as a pre-emptive strike, and with its light of invention, and other fortifications, dangle it as bait before some lowbrow publisher. Added to that, there was of course viragowatch.

That dilemma I still hadn't resolved when at six I tuned the radio for news. That, astonishingly, dwelt on Hugo as the last and most important issue in the train of these others: the Iraq election; the PM's projected tenure of Number 10; a building in Madrid on the brink of collapse; the Pope, after his recent hospitalisation; some nasty jibes against a Jewish journalist (notable because mayoral). The last trailing item centred on the scandal surrounding the deceptively mild-mannered Hugo Blythe, where just a trace of exuberance, in the news hack doing the interview, succeeded wonderfully, masking the more usual triumphalism the BBC reserves for these occasions. Hugo was able to state, categorically, that although he enjoyed the odd aperitif, he *was not* an alcoholic – rehabilitated or otherwise. On the question of Lemuel – no, he did not consort with violent criminals, nor offered them succour. Evidence suggested – and not to him alone – a tragic miscarriage of justice – though he'd add no more than that, in its current state of process. Oh – then what about his Europhobic tendencies? All you in the media, he ticked his interlocutor off, have never made Europe a ground for sensible discussion. For the record, his own position was roughly that of the Prime Minister's. Europe was our future, but not without reform. The question was, was Europe capable of reform?

The conclusion didn't necessarily follow the premise. When asked if there was truth in the rumour he'd offered to resign, Hugo said stiffly there was – which of course implied he *had* done something wrong.

February 15 What threatened to be the derailment of my plans was a phone call, just as I debated how best to time re-entry into the office, to clear my desk. Aim was an air of understated fortissimo charging the atmosphere, and methodical detachment in the simple act of going through my drawers. Sadly our daily politics made no provision for that martyrdom. Hugo called me at last, re-tensioning – this time for my capture – the same snares the PM had set for him, with a personal interdict barring my resignation. Hugo even suggested that in cultivating the right sense of insouciance, gains were possible, with the narratives of rival power apt to negate their own point of closure – a coded Gallic lingo sounding dubious to me, philosophically. One couldn't help wonder what harlequinade he envisaged both of us performing in. I therefore asked him what he understood by my position, reminding him that not only a part of my diary, but all of it as it now stood, was in Tamara's hands.

'Well what else is in it?'

I told him cryptic notes, incomprehensible lists, bits and pieces culled from the internet, jottings I'd made, personal musings – all of which was strictly speaking not the truth. That however was less a worry than the encroachment on my time that remaining in post equated to – one of all kinds of incidental evils he was forcing me to contemplate. I felt this huge reluctance, was all I could say, and couldn't foresee dropping in to the office more than once or twice a week.

'Oh now Al why take that view?'

'Isn't it obvious? I've got to get this diary out before Tamara does.'

'I can't approve of that.'

'Are you sure, Hugo? One more blunder and you *will* be asking me to go.'

He put up less than robust resistance, and furthermore, provided I engineered only a good press from this day forth – a good press for him – he offered to have materials sent over and facilities installed (I've got a webcam and the like).

Hours dragged. There isn't much you can do when palpable unrest, if it won't fully reveal itself, darkens your interiors. That was a cue for Robert Hailer too, who bleary-eyed and late at night had caught the rolling news, and had seen the Blythe interview, replayed for the nth time across the TV universe. He emailed, and with reference to Lem joked that if his own position deteriorated he'd knock on Hugo's door in Kentish Town, and plead for asylum. That took me aback, as now I began to wonder if all that walled Utopia, from almost a week ago (February 9), was a fiction – and that the true motivation in his disinterment process was to recall in poetic terms the exquisiteness of youth. As he explained, that might always be a poet's underlying project. Youth remains a tantalising shore, while the shipwreck of adulthood, in its ceaseless collision with the world, is a vastness of no one person's making, random in its changes. Rural as his Wiltshire idyll was, this pacifying lyric I so looked forward to wasn't its automatic corollary. And wasn't there always something bleak and threnodic about words and music rooted in the soil?

'Don't tell Seamus Heaney.'

With everything bound to its mesmerising opposites, his newest sequence of poems, the ink barely dry on the manuscript still in his windy garret, centred on the perfections of family life, from the advertising viewpoint. First stock character is the happy father, who blinks instantly awake on the sound of his alarm, and afloat beneath his duvet beams with dental precision, unalloyed in its whiteness. His looks are Mediterranean. So are his pretty wife's. Sunshine fills their bedroom, a pure gold that only brightens when their two adorable children – a boy and a girl, similar in age – tumble in and jest around. So it runs, through the breakfast ritual, cereals soaked in milk, toast a crisp, burnished brown, served with abundant mail, bearing every kind of news (if there are bills, so what!). I didn't discourage him. What did haul him in was how late it was, so that the drive to work, and the skip to school, brought him to an abrupt halt, moments short of a mythological nine a.m. Just as he got going, too.

'Looking forward to the next instalment,' I said.

February 16 Today's first pause in the sequence of office intrigue is recorded at 11.23 a.m., the moment I sipped at a mug of parsnip soup, while at the same time saving to disc the sizeable attachment (in excess of a hundred kilobytes) Emma dispatched with her latest emailed woes. She describes a wrapped-up, hatted stroll across the hotel lawn and into the village streets, primed for yet another disappointing conversation with McBride. Some of the detail I cannot interpret. But I am clear about the sense of irony her mounting frustration has brought about. It's unusual for her, and a strange new phenomenon her colleague affected not to notice. At one point she quipped that with the unearthing of a pre-war centime it was possible to peddle it as just one more in a chain of syntagms traceable as far back as you liked, even to dualistic practices in Christian-era southern France, a proposition that stirred in McBride a second school of phantoms, encouraged that at last his intellectually beautiful famulus had entered into the spirit of things. He thought she might even have discovered new depths of meaning in the idea of national currencies. I can only imagine Emma's nightmare. Like Hailer she is spending much of her time upstairs – in her case as self-exile – devoting more and more of her time to articulating her thoughts – and not for my benefit alone. Her rummage is through the failures of Thalia Jardyne, whose decades-long leadership hasn't saved the world from opportunists, men like Professor McBride.

Here was a version of her thesis, a distraction, and here was my parsnip soup, looking less and less attractive, lukewarm and turning cold. Let me add a note of caution, and confess that feminist literature is a commercial genre I take only a sporadic interest in. I cannot claim more than a few tentative question marks, one or two neutral exclamation points, in the margins of Emma's joust with Thalia Jardyne. She resists the accusation levelled at those of her followers Jardyne sees as having blunted her crusade. My neighbour from across the landing, who at all times has been perfectly polite with me, senses a profundity she might have overlooked, with those of her sisters protesting she's gone too far. Not all in her army rise to the high ground in TV or radio studios, or the ethers of paper publishing or academe, and must therefore co-ordinate their strategy in a much less glamorous theatre of combat, i.e. the dreary world of work. I mean, look at Avril. For Emma the Jardyne invective amounts to betrayal, when all she can lead her minions to is the same neurosis suffered by working men, who find themselves saddled with mortgages and with home responsibilities, and are broken by the lures of material acquisition. Moreover she didn't think men were as Jardyne described them, obsessed daylong with video games and masturbating every half an hour. They were like McBride – lost and wanting to be found.

Betrayal also underpinned those puritanical pronouncements sometimes heard in the liberal Jardyne, who rejects as one of the 'nobodies' any young adult or intern who takes her bedroom opportunities in pursuit of her career, with hand or oral favours given out in office hours. I cannot imagine Emma having offered herself so, though she views Jardyne's proscription of them as conceding that worldly success belongs to the entitled. That, she says, is one more postulate borrowed from the handful of men who ran the world, which did not include our glorious PM. Nor did it sit well with earlier mantras, when the process of assimilation was far from proof of liberation, given that her ideal was the assertion of difference. (So what, Emma asks, is the difference between an unfree man and an unfree woman?) Alaric Casteele is the last to say he knows. Emma hints that probably she does, and thinks that so must Thalia, but can't afford to damage her position. Alas there were always contras buckling her pen with every book she wrote. So there we are, Ms Thalia Jardyne, an unfree woman you are, no more divested of acculturation practices than the rest of us. The worst paradox of all, or so Emma muses, is the more you deconstruct, the more like a misogynist she is.

Then of all standing monuments the one un-garlanded in Thalia's lexicon of war is the phallus (of course), and by that I mean Emma's 'of course' (Al has absolutely no say in this). My correspondent asks, has what follows become a cliché? A well-trodden phrase, as common as our morning mail, and allowed to settle, wholly unchanged, on the bookish highways Jardyne and others ply their trade along? Emma suspects that the binarism 'penetration / domination' has evolved into one of those tautologies no one now evaluates as such, and is a consequence of a long chain of associations incidental to the patriarchal order the centuries have wrought. If conversely all commerce between the sexes had arisen via the reverse, matriarchal blueprint, Emma can envisage the act of coitus, construed in its masculine psychology, as an act of servility – we downtrodden males dispensing pleasures in a hedonistic female world. She thinks she has supporting data for that view, confessing privately to long, agonised, one-to-one discussions with Anna's departed spouse, a man necessarily anonymous, whose shattered ménage I am anxious not to inherit. Quaintly, the climax of his breakdown is described in visceral terms, where the conjugal bed has long gone cold, and what demands he does express render him dirty and disreputable. The point arrives where he ceases to ask. As far as Emma knows, Thalia Jardyne has never known a long-term relationship, let alone borne children, and so puts at jeopardy her projected place in history, what with all these half-formed insights.

About that I wouldn't know. And there are things that Emma doesn't know – for example how, without statistics, to counter Jardyne's unassailable declaration that here, in our servant economy, it is womenfolk who do the 'vast majority' of unattractive, unprotected jobs. Characteristic of this powerfully influential author is selective citation of sources apparently.

I'm bound, Emma, to return to this.

February 17 Can't help but think that Hugo is less than sanguine about these current activities of mine. This morning he sent me a motorcycle courier, a man who, in every awkward combination, rattled the ironmongery of my outer door, and kept to its tuneless interlude for as long as I took to abandon my computer screen and open up. That I did with undisguised abruptness. The man, mildly gigantic – as everyone my junior seems to be – bore himself with all that intimidation a surly English education endows, symptomatic of expanding populations in a highly competitive era. In the short charged silence through which he returned my gaze only his crepitating leathers communicated anything. I couldn't fail to note the capacious, decorated helmet nestled under his arm, and a large parcel of papers at his feet, for me evidently, in a binding I later hacked at with my bread knife. As I might appreciate, no words were needed (therefore why waste breath?). A covering note from Hugo said 'Please attend to all of these,' a task calculated to take me several days, and which I countered by phoning a few choice newspaper people, with whom I entered into certain negotiations. Hugo's paperwork I didn't give a second thought to. Instead I worked solidly till ten p.m., the approximate moment that Anna phoned, eager with excitement when, with barely a speck of dust having settled since her final interview, she'd been offered a job. The firm was public relations, with offices in Goodge Street, whose client list – according to its website, which I later went and looked at – included the England football team and the executors not of one but two dead rock stars. One fell to various addictions, the other was AIDS-related. The pressures of public life.

'Wonderful news,' I said.

'Isn't it!'

A first insistent image was an animated Anna in the small square hall of her house, whose only phone was on a semi-oval table top, she with the door ajar to her lounge, its furnishings lively with firelight, and twirling a pencil through her hair. She tried to hush her words, having shooed Charlotte up to bed. In small places voices floated up the stairs. These ambient conditions she had managed to get under close control, so I was honoured with a half-hour monologue, thoroughly rehearsed, and uttered *sotto voce* to its first patient hearer, a man whose occasional ums could not conceal his interpretation of her situation. Momentous they might have been, yet these options she now had to consider were a dilemma. She said she thought she would, then that she thought she wouldn't commute. The one problem with that was the early-morning starts, with a return to the hearth close to Charlotte's bedtime. Other, troubling complications involved the goodwill of friends, which you couldn't take for granted if, for an indefinite period, routine childcare, including car rides to and from school and out-of-school activities, was necessary. Charlotte had her ballet class, and twice a week she swam, and Anna wouldn't want to compromise any of this.

A more radical approach was selling her tiny cottage and a return to London, with all that entailed. Rank, for now she stratified herself, coupled with affordability, was going to mean a poky little flat, and a leafless street, and one of those tormented neighbourhoods urban centres replicated everywhere. She'd have to find a school. Then of course friends in a new neighbourhood were not easy to make, if you had to work all day. Her third option was one I couldn't feel comfortable with, gestated as it was on assumptions I didn't think she ought to make. First among these was Emma as landlady (hard to imagine), her spare room 'automatically' available for rent, and ideal while Anna made more permanent arrangements. I was too close at number 7 should that be agreed on, and eventually go wrong.

'When,' I asked, 'is your start date?'

'March – middle of.'

'Oh, no panic then. There's plenty of time….'

February 18 I note how my patterns of behaviour are formed by my radio scheduling. One advantage in spending so much time at home is this mechanical, day-to-day selection process applied to the rolling acreage of broadcast information. I discover that the dull, plummy newsman, whose dreary intonation has punctured my little English universe over years of six-o'clock bulletins, specialises in the Scottish Enlightenment. Offered the right vehicle – in this case a fifty-minute documentary – the man touches electrifying heights when given *laissez-faire* with Adam Smith and David Hume. This morning, another arrival at the lectern was an acquaintance of mine, whose epithet – well known in the corral of books and media – was the formal R. J. Baines, though he's Rodders to me (and not related to Alan Baines). I knew he'd spent time working in Singapore, Hong Kong, Auckland, but now he was back on home turf (at UCL), and had returned with one of his papers to deliver on air. Today it was Jeremy Bentham, and a legacy in Utilitarianism I could have made good use of had I written this diary in a less curmudgeonly way. *Mea culpa.*

Rodders and I go way back. What occasion it was I can't remember, but my first encounter was as tetchy undergraduate. It was a birthday, or similar anniversary. The rite is immaterial. What mattered were my pious friends, long lost by now, who in the end would wish I hadn't been invited. In the first place I hated the venue, a posh elitist eatery, trading on a classic name I now forget, a place self-conscious and not at ease, located on the High (near Carfax), and over-zealous in its bright, recent refurbishment. My best refuge was a good vintage port, lethal in its combination with the soapbox I got up on. R. J. Baines, a rising star on the academic circuit, had been pointed out at a nearby table. Over on our tables, the narrow range of topics, with its accent on student life, anecdotal as that might be, was under stewardship of someone I deplored, generous host though he was. It was a tense, exploratory exchange. I tired of its etiquette, breaking its wicked spell only accidentally, having waved away the cheeseboard, and in fiery inattention tipped over someone's wine – a lapse in co-ordination whose result was a crimson stain in the pristine starch of the tablecloth. I couldn't say I cared, and with the tinkle of nervous laughter that followed I emptied a saltcellar – a very tidy pyramid it made – on the offending spot. Cued at the graceless, transformational effect all of this produced, I peppered the conversation with comments verging on the boorish. Bloke whose wine I'd spilt looked at his wristwatch, and rather than wait for its golden chime claimed he'd got work to do, and left, having gently folded his napkin. The waiter returned and mopped up the mess, though I sent him back to the bar, now that my own glass was empty. One other in our party left, followed by two more, whose coats took too long to find, a delay that left them looking ashen when they did emerge.

From there I descended further into the volcano I had made, launching into any damning critique, the target arbitrarily chosen, and not precisely focused under my intoxicated aim. Neither my friends nor R. J. Baines rose to this awful challenge, though the latter quietly wished me goodnight when – finally left alone at my table – I watched him also leave the restaurant. I met him again, in the open air in London, in the following summer – it was the solstice – amazingly by chance. We drank a sober lemon tea under the awning of one of the park cafés, the place untroubled by traffic, but loud with street noise nonetheless. He recalled I had shown my ignorance of the work of some philosopher or other, whom I'd sounded off about back on the High. (You see, I have always been like this.) I now vaguely remembered having rubbished certain theories, but that was all I admitted to. He said nevertheless I had raised one or two interesting points, which he urged me to put more lucidly – a dangerous prospect, given Baines's reputation as a philosopher. I declined humbly, smiling as gently, as patiently as I might.

Since then the prolific R. J. Baines has been a permanent entry in my address book, though after his journeys east we did not stay in touch. I shall have to track him down now that he's returned. I shall have to let him know I'm looking for a job, and need some introductions. But oh now who's that on the phone…?

It was Anna.

February 19 Hugo rang me from his surgery, and wants to know how I'm getting on with that filing cabinet of papers left me on Thursday (February 17). I told him I'd better things to do. This morning that better thing was one of my regular visits to viragowatch, where I learned that my manuscript had been scanned to disc, and is in transit, one to another in Uttoxeter Street, where some of the cryptic secret language I've employed it is Avril's job to work into damaging sentences. This is exactly why I've got no time. Hugo emailed later in the day, to let me know how dispiriting his re-election campaign is turning out to be. He really does wish I'd wade through all that paperwork, which he claims is directly related to this problem.

'I can understand the electorate's changing attitudes to the war,' he says, 'but how can that one issue influence all others?'

'Well, Hugo, it's like this…'

February 20 Hugo again, insisting I apply myself to his current problems (as if I'm not already). Very well, Hugo, this is how it is:

even the most disengaged, and the most distant from you socially, fully understand the necessity of political dishonesty. In your case I would sum this up as two divergent views, the public and personal, which whatever mask you wear you cannot reconcile. To take some examples, how, Hugo, would you have dealt in *Risposta* with some of the following, and what do you say about them on the doorstep now? We'll take them alphabetically—

Amnesty International
Anglican Church, The
Archbishop of Canterbury
Arts funding, high and low
Asylum seekers

Bank of England, The
Bollywood

Campaign Against ID Cards
Chancellor of the Exchequer,
  The
China, People's Republic of
Chong, Annabel
Commonwealth Games, The

Education, education,
  education
Ethnic tensions
Eugenics
Europe

Family values
Feminism
Football
Frankfurt School
Funding for the BBC

Genetic screening
Global capitalism
Global warming

Greenpeace
Gulf wars past and present

Hollywood
House of Lords

Immigration
Inner-city deprivation
Internet discussion forums

Jardyne, Thalia

Kennedys, The
Kyoto Agreement

Liberal Democrats, The
Liberty (the campaign group)

Man Booker Prize, The
Marriage and role reversals
Marx, Karl
Media and public careers
Mitchener, Anton

'New men' of the Nineties
Nuclear industry

Orange Prize, The
Oxbridge novelists

Performance poets

Lots of course I've missed.

February 21 These days work begins as soon as the rising winter sun ripples my bedroom drapes, and is carried on with every notch around that dial, and farther still into the cold shadows of late afternoon or evening. Once I've felt that chill I stroll around my republic, turning on table lamps, and closing curtains on another night of toil. Tonight I took my fatigue into the unearthly silence of my living room, just as I did almost exactly a month ago, and at the window glanced down into the street, where a soft dejected porch light broke as a crumpled triangle across a station wagon, neatly double parked. A man in noisy leather boots and a lightweight outdoor fleece, with a riot of silver hair, stepped out and opened the boot, from which he unladed two sturdy travel bags. When the boot lid went down, Emma, whom I hadn't seen emerge from the passenger side, was standing beside him, with her purse open, and her cold marmoreal hand clutching at its banknotes. She was garbed plainly in a long, knitted cardigan, which swept to her ankles but didn't seem to keep her warm. Her driver took both bulky cases to the doorstep, one at a time. While his client looked for her key he was seized by a change in posture, and offered defensive-looking gestures as she spoke. I couldn't hear the reply, though the sentiment was clear, and I knew – even before he'd got back in the car – that he wouldn't be hauling her bags to the landing. She paid him, and he drove off – three terrific over-revs, and as many ascents through the gears. I twitched the nets and turned my back, and went downstairs.

'Emma, you're back! Let me help you with those things….'

'Al! So nice to see a friendly face….'

I thought she looked well, despite her tribulations with McBride, who, she said, was piqued at her decision to come home. As ever their final exchange was in the open air, where with commendable rein on his anger McBride bludgeoned his spade into a frozen clod of earth, and snapped the shaft in trying to lever to the surface what hidden treasures he imagined there. I resisted a smile, and carried her cases in and left them in her hall, then followed her to the kitchen, where with journalistic dreariness I described that long succession of events arising from the burst in her water main, and how I'd placated Alf downstairs, etc. She turned the main back on and adjusted the strand of hair that had curled across her cheek. Both of us watched, a little sceptical perhaps, she with her thin shoulders angled over the draining board, until at last the cold tap wheezed then spluttered into life, then jetted torrents into the sink. She filled her kettle for a cup of tea and turned the central heating on.

'Em, you should have told me you were coming. I'd have got the place ready.'

'Frankly, Al, didn't make my mind up until this morning.'

Barring the few tins she kept – for nuclear and other disasters – there were no provisions in her stores, so very gallantly I led her the short walk to my dining table, where I resurrected the vegetable stew I'd spooned into freezer bags just a few nights before. I had also, a day or so old, a *bâtard* I'd bought from the local *boulangerie*, which after five minutes under a low oven heat returned to an edible state. She waived the coffee course, feeling tired, and here the conversation flagged, which suited me, as now we'd begun to talk about Anna's latest plans – a topic I found it easy to deflect.

The phone rang later when I too was feeling tired and wanted to go to bed. It was Hugo. What I shall say now is in retrospect, of course, as I know how unforgiving I can be when the day is overlong and Morpheus stalks the shadows. Yet, I could not help detect, in the euphoria in Hugo's voice, another of those deceits I had learned to recognise from working in his office. He'd looked at my list, he said (see February 20, immediately above), and declared it so ingenious on my part that – given the right context (which I *had* been careful to give him) – it was possible to understand its dualistic or even duplicitous nature.

'How so, Hugo?' I asked.

He rattled off all the proper nouns, except, portentously, the most important to his social wellness at this critical time. That one he thought to stifle further in showing how pleased he was that if ever questioned publicly, his critique on human industry was always an enlightened one, from Marx to Annabel Chong.

'Ah yes,' I said. 'But what about Jardyne?'

Here that euphoria turned to the matter-of-fact. Far from boast that this was politically astute, he was pleased to have postponed his appearance on *Soapbox Sentinels* several times (though so had Jardyne). His ground would always be safe so long as he avoided hectoring plants in the audience and the menace of Thalia's eruptions, which as we both knew she had a weakness for when in sight of a camera. I was not encouraged. I couldn't resist Machiavellian interventions. I reminded him that all manner of damaging material was leaking from our office, part of the reason I wasn't any longer there. How did he know some cloaked malicious person wasn't tracking each revised pen stroke in his official diary and passing that information to Thalia herself?

'Oh come on, Al, that's preposterous!'

I allowed a little pause. Then he asked about my researches into that person.

'I've got someone working on that, Hugo. You want me to call her off?'

No, was his reply.

February 22 For motives I dwelt on only superficially, Robert Hailer troubled to let me know that a new business arrangement had brought him back to London. Where that was in the vast metropolis he didn't say, though his lodgings he was less evasive about: location a cheaply decorated boarding house, gleefully serving beer and breakfasts all day long, with every homey corner soaked in satellite TV. He was after my advice, asking that since he was here for a couple of days, was it worth his while to attend Hugo's talk tonight? I asked myself what talk, and couldn't admit to Hailer – he and I fellow-pariahs – that the level of mutual suspicion existing between the minister and his researcher meant I knew nothing at all about this. I checked all the obvious agencies online, and discovered that yes, in the Boothroyd Room, Portcullis House, Hugo was blabbing on with something he'd called 'Why the Arts and Politics Need Each Other'. What a huge waste of time that will be.

The question I couldn't resolve was how he could contemplate further subjection to party propaganda, recalling as I did that last exchange we had on February 9. Those lines he quoted to me then I've tried to place, in the odd spare moment, ever since, but now, finally, I've remembered. They belong to that quasi-theological phase and *Off the Party Ecliptic*, a book I re-referred to. One of its poems is titled 'A Declaration'. Under present considerations, it's worth reproducing—

> Now the certainties had passed: the reign
> of holy strife, the giving and taking away,
> the preachers and the patriarchs, had been
> removed. Here, the fighter had stood, his weapons
> raised against the heavens, his heavy shoulders
> turned against the world, his time arriving.
> Here before the Party faithful he renounced their human
> god, and challenged each new certainty. 'In a hope or political
> prayer,' he said, 'responsibility is never really mine, my days
> are sacrificed to imaginary fraternities, our social incapacities
> are urged to improvement in a blanket mediocrity.'
> But it wasn't that, as someone counted grains
> of sand. Our fighting rebel knew – as we all knew –
> that in those grains of sand the self-righteous had been roused.

In a creeping realisation that, if the lounge in his boarding house offered just a continuous loop of soccer goss, hosted by a newly rinsed anchorman and woman – two persons hinting they'd got stuff on the players' wives – then the idea of Hugo Blythe, under weight of liberal left ideals, probably did seem more attractive.

'I'll see you there,' I said.

For some reason the organising bureaucracy had gone for an early, 6.30 start. Despite that the event was well attended. I arrived as one of the stragglers. I took my seat and scanned for the most likely candidate fitting Hailer's profile. All I had to go on was the inset portrait on the reverse cover of *Off the Party Ecliptic*, done in monochrome, under well-adjusted lighting. The drawback was its era, the book belonging to – and in every sense not escaping – a decade long gone. Added to that you're either cynical, as I am, or remotely accepting, knowing how public relations and photo imaging combine in the same misleading canvas. Then of course the shot, I imagine at the discretion of his agent, picked from an over-stuffed portfolio, was five years out of date (even way back then). So the deception perpetuates itself, to the very moment of mechanical reproduction. But, anyway, enough of that. What *did* he look like all those years ago? Well, slightly aristocratic, with an old-world, public-school haircut, his ears oversized, bright, intelligent eyes, and a firm, beautifully sculpted lower lip. The smile was a winning smile, and the chin was moderately weak.

Hard as it was to extrapolate – from the aspic of ancient airbrushed features, to the living persona now – I settled on three contenders. All were men of about my age, one with collapsed cheeks and roguish hair, another with silvery quiffs and cherry-coloured lips, and a greying, outdoor-looking type, wearing a heavy greatcoat, and clutching a broad-brimmed leather hat to match. This latter seemed least at odds with what I'd envisaged, for is it not the case that expectancy lightens everything? The other two I gradually ignored, and it was on him, in increased certainty, that my gaze often, briefly, fell. I couldn't fail to note how he scrolled hypnotically through the menu of his mobile phone, and wasn't at ease. Hugo meanwhile made his polite introductions at the lectern, where he'd appeared jacketless, and now poured himself water from a small carafe. He opened on a note of levity, unusual for him, and asked what in the present age we made from the following disclosure. That disclosure I inferred implicated me, if only indirectly. What he referred to was the recent vacancy he'd sought to fill on his research team, and how one applicant listed her interests as follows—

> Art, travel, photography, philosophy, literature, poetry, writing, museums, film, ashram retreats, androgyny, feminism, strong women, beautiful minds, affection, antique furniture, Victorian dress, corsets, Middle-East and Indian cuisine, belly dancing, autumn and winter, nature, Eastern cultures, Hindu temple structures, Byzantine and Islamic architecture, cafés, wine, ritualistic percussion, Eastern thought, Indian folk dance, interior design, yoga, impassioned, exotic song.…

Hailer was grim-faced throughout this litany. However, according to Hugo, the serious point to be made was measured not in the list itself, but in the breadth of mentality capable of its articulation. In *his* assessment here was the gemstone of our nationhood in urgent need of defence, so to speak played off against the xenophobic headlines met with daily in a scurrilous tabloid press, doing its best to wipe its shine and sweep it aside. (One wonders why Hugo hadn't recruited said applicant, rather than the much more conservative Alaric Casteele – a question I shall one day put to him.) Anyway, the rest of his address failed to meet the anticipated climax of his opening remarks. In fact he droned to the point of tedium, through a thesis Hailer didn't get to the end of, because of that mobile phone. All of us heard its muffled chime under the gigantic pleats of his greatcoat, followed by a shrilling Diabelli variation number one as he put it to his ear. He stumbled out. If this did turn out to be him, I didn't expect us to meet today.

But unexpectedly I found him, out on the cobbles when, later, I too left the building. His hat was slanted rakishly over one eye, and conversation through his cell phone was heated enough that his coattails were airborne. I waited for an appropriate lull, then I said to him 'You're Robert Hailer.'

February 23 It was well past the time we'd agreed, but I called on Robert Hailer at his boarding house. The delay was just one more thing I apologised about, which in a chunter to myself I blamed on the locality, a rundown town, whose every road was the same, which for reasons impossible to fathom Hailer was staying in. A warren of distant streets I drove in endlessly – a solid cold monotony – with every changing suburb sliding by in an ugly blur of ancientness. Hailer had got the suite of rooms that his landlord, a man rotund, jolly and snarling, claimed had been occupied by Daniel Defoe, that author travelling north in 1722 (for him a productive year). Not so hard to imagine. There was a slope to the floor, a dip that reached its lowest point as you entered. The walls were uneven, which no amount of filler had straightened. There was a plastic beige cover for the table, where Hailer sat by his window, its surface a medley of assorted objects orbiting his hat. These were: a rose-coloured candle stub, fixed to the upturned lid of a supermarket jar, set in the wax of its own eruptions; a hand mirror whose clear unblemished silver doubled the razor blade at rest on its horizontal surface; two sizeable tomes, one a critical appraisal of Angela Wryle, who was one of his supplanting poets at EUP, the other a Chambers biographical dictionary, bookmarked severally; and an empty can of stout, stoved in below the shoulders. There was some cheap-looking whisky, its bottle more than half consumed.

We drank coffee and, as hypothetically as I might, I urged him to find a reviewer for his *Razor Manifesto*, on the less than certain understanding that with favours owing, support through the pages of *Risposta* ought to be a possibility. The conversation flagged. I glanced up at his coat hanging on the door. Hailer fingered then picked up one of those two books (the critique), and with an eyebrow raised read me a not so random passage. I make no effort whatsoever to recover its exact wording, and I shan't be investing library time or money through my bookshop – either virtual through my PC screen, or in that concrete entity with its disintegrating pitch out on the High Street – and report only on the textual appropriations Hailer was so incensed by in his enemy. The language of combat he said had been his own, self-conscious in its metaphor, aimed at rounding in on itself that less than regal legacy of popes, kings, generals, whose rampage through the centuries had formed the indelible stamp on the world as it comes to be at present. Here as a part of that evolution was a florid, seedy-looking Robert Hailer, aware of how absurd was the mere idea of gallantry, yet insistent it didn't exempt poets from the sacred duty only poets could perform. This I felt was uncomfortable territory, and I put it to him that regardless of the ethics of the situation, these sallies and outbursts persons of greater influence than mine would always filter through today's gender realignment. Given his state as casualty, a selfish rather than sacred motive was my understanding of his calling. That he said was the double exclusion he suffered. Not only was there nowhere he could go. His stock vocabulary, after an act of confiscation, was now clumsily redeployed in the war against him.

If I wasn't already reminded of the general tone and atmosphere of *Off the Party Ecliptic*, he corrected that omission now, in an awkward rendition of the book's closing plaint, a lyric climaxing the thirty-odd preceding, which like them mourned some grandiose passing on, a departure he supposed might as well have been his own. Perhaps it was explained in the closeness of the scrutiny I paid him – that over-mechanical motion of his jaws, or the mobile flab of his jowls – or perhaps it was his audience of one – not the rooms-full he'd known in previous decades. Anyway, the timbre was wood, the delivery staccato, the thrust embarrassed. He tried to explain that with obsessive procedures in correctness, all representatives of the ancient order he belonged to had been ejected from the debate, a cleansing process that if rigidly secular nevertheless had the same intensity theologically as all those religious purges besmirching centuries past. But, he got no further than that, as his phone rang, so that now he unhooked it in the corner he'd got it recharging in. Further, he answered his caller only in the room adjoining, where another heated exchange recalled the one I'd accidentally stumbled on at Portcullis House. Whatever the grand narrative, in the end the daily round must always take precedence.

I stumbled out, and in the dampish gloam, and the first amber flicker of roadside streetlights, I reversed my car from where I'd been forced to park it several streets away, and swung out immediately into the first of many wrong turns. From here I was caught in a long depressing thread of taillights, a procession snaking uphill endlessly, at the crown of whose summit a set of traffic lights, under the glaze of rainwater, was almost permanently set to red. There, eventually, my instincts failed altogether, and of the three place names signposted, I opted for the one I was least familiar with, for I remembered none from the outward journey, and this, irrationally, clinched it. With that and further stuttering decisions, other drivers took their chance. A cab, later a delivery truck, then a pantechnicon all cut across my nearside from junctions I hadn't suspected. I turned on my wipers. Then the radio, which promptly I switched off. The next sign I saw told me I was heading back for Hailer's guesthouse, a prospect filling me with such awful sadness I pulled in behind a bus and got to grips with the A to Z. Where I'd gone wrong was (but no, enough).

February 24 I don't begin to record the fractured whirl of nightmares yesterday's events have given rise to, whose first evil glimmers entered my waking consciousness only as I passed the doctor on the stairs. By the time I reached the corner shop the vision had resolved itself as fully as it could, a crazy cinematic footage stacked to studio height with just those petty conflations one is apt to puzzle over all day long. For example, here was a Lem I knew as really Hailer, off limits in a crumbling suburb, camped in a guesthouse actually a warehouse, the place a store for piecrust table tops and other domestic furnishings. You know how perplexing it always is. You never quite relate these dream creations to the solid events they index, and certainly yesterday's exchange, discounting the interruption of his cell phone, I hadn't felt was in any way uneven. There was on the other hand that inept recitation of his poem, which, as the clue to Hailer's disjointed mental landscape, I examined on the page—

'It looks as though this shrine means nothing
to him now. A monument constructed more to celebrate
a misconception than a principle.'

'Ah yes, the scene
of one who dreamed. Of one who at the end has paced
the streets at night, and in the briefest moment
is stripped of everything he values most.
But still alone? Look carefully, and tell me
what is there....'

'The irony of unconnected lives
that inhabit the remote and independent
islands of the universe. Of the many thousands
their inventiveness conceives, one currency is set apart,
and raised to unimagined heights to regulate the passing
of their days.

'But that is awkward
now, these few uneasy steps beyond the utmost corner
of his life, where he flings abuse up here, his unlit
heaven. Death, the undiscovered country. Life,
the unrewarded, arbitrary chore. The desolation
of the spheres.'

'A cry as long and silent as in the end
the new theology lays bare.'

I suppose a problem the reading public always has with grand, universal themes, and the books about them, is their doubtful application in a changing social world, which was one of those authorial perplexities I might have considered in more depth, had Emma not gently tapped at my door. She was looking tired, and dejected, and by the time I opened up her hands were deep in the pockets of her cardigan, in the frozen act of folding that blue garment round herself. Nor was there much of the usual lustre in her eyes, though the first thing she wished to say was her life at home was back to its routine (apparently that was good). Perhaps it was nothing personal, and all I saw in her waifish figure here in my draughty porch was down to that everlasting shiver of English winter.

'Emma, you look – pale….'

She said she'd like the receipts and paperwork charting that cascade of minor house repairs to hers and the flat below. I told her that could wait until the insurance claim, but she was adamant, insistent: her chequebook was open on her kitchen table, and she wanted to settle up.

'Okay. Now let me see.'

It took me half an hour, as other drains on my attention kept me at the computer, or gassing on the phone. But, I bundled everything together and slipped it in a file, and having made my apologies sat under the cold fluorescent light of Emma's kitchen, trying to remember what repair belonged to what illegibly handwritten invoice. As she wrote out my cheque I could not help but remark on the wodge of estate agents' details also on the table, near her writing hand.

'Not moving, Emma?' I said.

'Not me, Al. Anna.'

Glad I was that the shock I felt at that news didn't register with her, as she didn't mind telling me how put out *she* was. It wasn't solely at having to gather property information. More onerous, Anna was planning on her and Charlotte camping out in Emma's flat while she looked around.

I browsed flippantly through what vendors' literature she'd collected, less detached than I should have been at its enthusiastic patter, a gloss of semi-truths reinforced by carefully framed photographs. They followed the same unlikely angles, through an artificial camerawork ballooning small bow frontages into classical façades, or transposing poky little interiors to the planes of grand or gracious living. Postage-stamp backyards had a meretricious alfresco Mediterranean look, under a luminous, autumn London sky. I consoled myself that Anna would never afford the stratospheric sums asked for these modest properties, but that didn't prevent me telling her sister – I relied on her to pass it on – that work with Hugo was almost at an end. I'd made decisions, and I was looking for an academic post, 'possibly at Sussex', where I still had contacts.

'So, Al, you're on the move….'

'It looks that way.'

February 25 I surprised everyone by calling at the office, at the lonely hour of noon, where with blatant big hellos for both former colleagues I logged onto viragowatch, and for sixty minutes looked busy with important toil. I also checked my mail (an intray full of dross), and binned every last shred of it. Wearily I scrolled through screens of other unsorted refuse, mostly Tamara to Avril and back, and found what I hadn't known I was looking for – viz., secret insights Imogen Sinclair had shown her friend the Arts Minister. She was aware that Hugo had intervened more than once with private calls to the chair of *Soapbox Sentinels*, postponing his appearance each time he'd learned the ferocious Jardyne had followed his example and also deferred. In the usual coarseness you associate with her trade, this had led her to speculate that threatened with Thalia's debating style Hugo was more than ever running scared. What he most sought to avoid was exposure of those misogynistic inclinations 'all of us' knew him for. Tamara, wiser than that, replied that so far as *her* analysis went, Hugo remained a closet gay, who did not wish to be outed.

February 26 Hugo is much in my thoughts today…

February 27 …and by sheer coincidence he phones. He tells me he has heard I stooped to appear in the office on Friday (February 25, above), and asks if this will now become a habit. He doesn't understand. There are two good reasons only for making my presence felt in Uttoxeter Street, and infrequently at that: I must keep Avril and Tamara in a state of incomprehension, but of greater weight I must be a good citizen and sift the mountainous wastes of accumulating paper into the recycle bin. I can't seem to impress on Hugo how enormous a labour this diary has become, and of course I can't tell him about viragowatch.codec, or have him incriminated with it. But, regarding that, a crucial stage has now been reached. This is because today I begin the task of visiting all its entries retrospectively, to decide which to copy, paste, edit, thence include as the clinching, damning deceits in a new political world all of us are vulnerable in. I must complete it urgently and put the thing up for auction before Tamara does the same with her version.

Yet all of these are asides, and are not why Hugo has rung. There are more press 'revelations', he says, so dutifully I stroll down to the local newsagent, where against my sense of honour I part with cash for the offending publication. I spend much of this evening glancing across at my dining table, where, casually, I tossed it down, but cannot bring myself to pick it up and start to read. Anyway much of my time is taken up arranging a crossing into France, as I think a few days in the gîte – without the phone – should give me the scope this final phase of progress needs.

February 28 Grudgingly I scan the news (the Sunday paper, yesterday), and find this time only vicarious snipes at Hugo, in a careful aim at me, allegedly the 'kind of researcher' the Minister for Cult likes to keep employed. I paraphrase, and by the way I'm no longer Alan Cassell – new epithet is Alastair Cass—

> '…a man wholly sad, for who in a healthy frame of mind would want to consort with that misogynist and broken poet Robert Hailer, an effete specimen these days, unable to think beyond a schoolboy association with, of all unlikely people, the Messiah' (December 30).… This same Alastair Cass has absolutely no regard for the colleagues he works with (because on New Year's Eve I dismiss the efficient Hayley as not much more than 'a serving maid'). I do to my credit correctly identify my lack of rapport with those I share an office with as 'not quite right', but this pales wretchedly as I scarcely raise a smile at the Christian festivities going on around me.

It's tedious, I know, but the thing goes on and on—

I am, I learn (January 4), somewhat 'flippant' when Hugo's underlying intolerance is rumbled by the press, and I belong with that offensive class of being who rummages through other people's bins (January 5). According to Imogen, this is symptomatic of Al's 'ineptitude' with modern life, an impression reinforced when, cloaked in his little world of espionage, I show my full small measure of old-style, static and unimaginative thinking in a refusal to acknowledge media technology as 'a tool of education' – and I do not view education itself as one of my boss's responsibilities. All this is revealed on January 11. On January 12 I am 'anti-family'. On the 13th it's a grim state of affairs when trust has broken down between a cabinet minister and one of his principal researchers. Alastair Cass and Hugo Blythe even lie to one another. On the 14th I'm a winebibber, while Hugo is less than complimented on his excellence in authorship.

What has all this to do with politics, you ask. Well…

…there are Hugo's malicious accusations against the prison system, though Imogen can't also resist 'confirmation' of that street brawl over piecrust table tops (January 15). As a corollary of that, in the strangest of all conflations, January 17 records my verbal threats issued over the phone. These are the depths I descend to once I have questioned the integrity of a 'highly regarded' and 'very distinguished official', employed by the CCRC. On the 18th I am construed as sympathetic to McBride, and seem not to regard as unethical the deception he works in recruiting Emma to his project (though neither McBride nor Emma is named). The day after that sees first signs that Cass will 'desert' his office – and by implication his duties too – in favour of a sybaritic life at home. When that becomes a bore, as it inevitably must, I am seen to break and enter into private property, whose only justification is a forlorn quest after my obsessions.

I am personally repulsive for other reasons too—

Hailer, whom I seem to admire so much, any rational being must dismiss as the enemy of pluralism (see January 20). It is therefore not surprising that, three days later, I show myself as someone harbouring enormous jealousy of those whose gifts enable them to talk about the arts on television. I am on the 24th typical of 'certain kinds of male', who conceive of gender issues not as a debate, but a war. On the 25th my job is described as a 'calling', but one I am completely indifferent to, to the point that I even describe my necessary paperwork as 'useless documents'. On this day too I am not above manipulating my friend and neighbour in Hugo's spiteful salvos aimed at Thalia Jardyne (though these are notional, in a kind of pre-emption of the Blythe / Jardyne encounter scheduled for *Soapbox Sentinels*).

I am lustful and brutish, because

…in face of what Imogen calls 'the family ideal', and a fortnight to the day after showing my contempt for that as an institution, I seduce a defenceless young woman – moreover one for whom I'm supposed to be doing a favour. On the day after that, the 27th, I show how horribly patronising a man like me can be with the women friends I do have.

The thing tails off in a ragbag of asides, implicating Hugo only once—

January 28: I admit that the 'lack of communication' between myself and Hugo leaves me directionless, while all the time the Minister runs his home as a safe house for the world's 'most vicious criminals'. January 29: Am 'damning' yet again of any aesthetic not my own (the car radio). February 3: Sadly, ever more committed to life away from the office. Unscrupulously, I even 'secure' consultancy working for a member of the opposition. February 4: Hatred of working people. February 6: Inclined to reduce weighty news matters below the rank of crossword puzzles.

It reads as a kind of school report, where pupil Cass really must do better.

March 1 There was only one thing I could do about these difficulties. I phoned Anna and told her that in all likelihood I would soon be working out of town, but in order to think things through had planned a few days in Breton (the gîte). I don't flatter myself with particular insight, social, psychological, or other, but I did register the changing pitch of her voice as symptomatic of just the conflict I'd intended. Confusion and curiosity vied with one another – and that meant panic. Then I had only to add to the torment, evading any hint at why I was leaving and where I expected to go. Any queries she had I forestalled, suggesting that she and Charlotte might also like a short holiday across the Channel. What followed was a predictable break in conversation, in whose short, oceanic pause these sudden decisions she had to make I could almost image. She asked herself questions I couldn't answer – for example, how long could she take Charlotte out of school? Then she'd have to re-think other arrangements she'd made. And a man was calling about the washing machine.

'Look, Anna, why not call me back….'

She took hours over that, but eventually responded, in a sanguine state of mind, so that all I had to do was tell her what time to be ready on Thursday afternoon, and I would pick them up. The ferry was from Dover.

'Don't forget your passports. I will do the rest.'

March 2 I rued the mistiming when, shortly after nine, Hugo had one of his minions connect us over the phone. Unusually, some useless patter while he picked up his extension was abruptly superseded by his brusque, urgent, artificial-sounding tone. He'd been forced, he said, to change his schedule for the next few days, the culmination of several months of canvassing on the part of the acronymic AWMA, not a string I am able to translate. Apparently it's one of those loosely defined pressure groups, hard at work politically on behalf of at least three distinguished film directors, all of them native to these shores. One such – famous as anybody can be, but a man I hadn't heard of – was hotfoot from Hollywood, where most of his work was done, and had arrived in London heading up a delegation whose expertise was investment – or how to word a plea for cash. I will not utter his name, a man enormously self-assured, but Hugo, not having that same confidence, and not familiar with his work, didn't wish to meet him in this present state of ignorance. He'd scoured the listings, and had found, in a distant conurbation south of the river, some fleapit currently showing the 'highly acclaimed' *Juventutis*.

'Highly acclaimed by whom?'

'Never mind that, Al.'

What I *was* expected to do, because after all I was, technically, still employed by Hugo, was muster up my equipage and journey into that hinter-country, whose tag was a south-east postcode. There under duress of my expense account I had licence to part with sterling, not so much to watch, but survey in every detail this *Juventutis*. Subsequently the report I filed, reaching him no later than Thursday, must carry concisely – i.e. not in my usual rococo – a full account of the following—

> Cast list
> Production team (including gaffer, best boy etc.)
> Scriptwriter and associates
> Location(s)
> Style, wardrobe department
> Hairdresser (it wasn't Helen Penfold)
> Aesthetic appreciation (that's to say *my* appreciation) re
>   camerawork, lighting (and do you really mean that, Hugo?)
> Special effects (if any)
> Plot, sub-plot, sub-sub etc.
> Message (political, social, other)

Instructions were not to leave this viewing for more than a couple of days, as the meeting had been pencilled in for breakfast time this Sunday. I pertly made it clear that this represented unacceptable wreckage to *my* plans. I had too much left to do, and I hadn't got much time, and as I was bound for the continent tomorrow I'd no choice but to abandon everything and set off on his wasted mission now. You may imagine what he said to that – I record, as a matter of indolence, few of the world's explosives and expletives. Grave as my misgivings were, I left with half a tank of fuel for what was listed as the matinée performance. The venue, a weathered brick building, was in a street only remotely implicated with my A to Z. I think had it not been for other traffic blurring through the rain – slow brown misshapes reducing all they cut across to half a trot – the sign would have missed me completely, a small inscription let loose in the mizzle awash above my eyeline. Then of course I couldn't park, and so left half the suburb bathed in my exhaust, in prelude of a first likely hectare looming in my windscreen. That, when at last it appeared, was a pocked macadam fenced off from the rest of the community. It lured me in to its waste and detritus: a mudguard, assorted hubcaps, an oil drum, the scattered remains of a breezeblock. I paid for two hours, having left my car tucked in innocently between a florist's small delivery van and a creamy blue Reliant.

Now the long walk under my umbrella. Then finally I tramped the steps up to the cinema foyer, where the star of *Juventutis* – a gallant even I could name – was there in cardboard cut-out, in permanent salutation. As a short, youthful, fortyish, many married man, and over-dressed for these parts (garb fit for Oscar night), he oversaw my ticket sale, and in all probability turned his young blue eyes towards the auditorium as I pushed open the door into that darkened womb.

What masque and charade did I witness there? Well now, Hugo, suspension of the collective psyche is a dreamed country, whose screen affairs are charmed (to a certain point), and where any initial introduction to it unveils floating cities lit with golden ligatures. The language uttered in that faery republic is recognisably our own. Some typical scenes are: California poolside, and the twinkle of ocean stars; lazy drives along the boulevards and up the hilly streets, which take us through dukedoms of moonlight; then there is its office life, with professional gals in thousand-dollar suits. One learns too, via other sensory means, how the suburbs, in an unremitting season, are fragrant with yellow oleander. The rub is, plunged into this pristine world are astute, commercial men of science, whose alloy labs are the seat of wonderful new industries. The wild-haired professor, with his hand tools, and his stone-cellar manias, is lost to the netherworld of melodrama, as are all those test-tube liquids always on the boil. Cue instead the corporate man of the boardroom or business park, trumpeting his creed. Technologically, and this we cannot fail to hear, this is the moment the elixir of youth is a concrete possibility. Truly, it's now a manufactured process, with a production line whose end is jars of brightly dotted pills. So, Hugo, for those of lesser rank like ours, this is bad news doubly. The investment costs alone – dollar signs as a cosmic radiation – will not permit the sale of any one pill for less than a month's salary. Paradoxically the adman's mantra is this: A pill a day rolls the years away.

A first clientele is the stars of Hollywood (this a self-reflexive film). Therefore that same reverse logic stunting all human progress is now a policy dictate. There can be few other mortals blessed with a wedge large enough to afford this assault on the ravages of age, or – their image already tyrannising over us – with a ready interest in the concept of immortality. So on through all depictions, the protagonist a man with fantastically swollen coffers, set for the repeat passage of twenty birthdays past, his life newly baptised at youth's eternal spring. Yet Hollywood wouldn't be Hollywood without its moralising cack. The Tom or Brad or Drew, whose icon stood cardboard sentry duty out by the box office, soon discovers that even eternity is transient. A new generation of consumers prefers its own temple of immortals, whose virtue may only be their difference – one more alluringly rugged perhaps, another more temperamentally angelic, a square not an oval face etc. Ergo Tom Brad Drew finds work less easy to come by. His fourteen mansions are reduced to one. His automobiles are auctioned off. All the leaves are brown. Image, once so integral to his salary-and-bonus scheme, is now the central problem, when with his addiction comes an ever-spiralling cost of the all-important elixir. At the same time his capacity to earn suffers an alarming and incommensurate decline. He's looking very *noir* by the time he turns to street crime, which as a proposition is Hollywood in regulation of itself. The message is, renewal is everything, and as a two-hour cinematic lecture it was one I could have done without. Let us hope the Chinese do much better once they are the primary power.

I left, and pushed on forward under the protection of my umbrella, a depressing little citizen slouching through a brown, angular drizzle. Back at my car, both the Reliant and the florist had gone, and were replaced on one flank only by a Jeep, its livery a battle grey and green (a conspicuous camouflage out here on the capital's disintegrating edge). Alas some roving *zanni* had taken the blade of a house or car key to the proud sheen of my sedan, and starting from the offside wing had left an incision in the paintwork, which ran in an unbroken horizon all the way to the rear indicator. Sì, ha-ha.

Drove home, filed my report, emailed it to Hugo.

March 3 An early start (a too early start). Even so, on the stroke of the radio pips for nine, and as I drew up at the picket fence fronting Anna's house, she'd already stacked her and Charlotte's luggage in the porch. Charlotte stood in profile at the lower window, brushing her hair, a chore she abandoned abruptly on hearing the purr of my engine. I parked, and attempted though could not summon a smile, as neither could she. Self-consciously she took herself off to another room.

I cut the engine and strolled up the narrow drive, and had barely reached the door when Anna threw it open wide. I made cursory observation as to the volume of baggage, and lifted the topmost from its pile.

'One more to come,' she said.

We loaded up, to the car's limits of suspension, and set off more or less at the time I'd planned. 'When are we going to be there?' was something Charlotte did not say. In fact we were among the first arrivals, cars in miniature snaking through the steel and concrete sprawled across the harbour. There in a light salty shower I nosed with care into the ferry's interior, with half an hour to go before departure. A glassy elevator took us to the upper decks, and a lounge where Charlotte chose a window seat. I put down my hand luggage and all of us looked out. Dockside, lots of flashing orange lights. Out to sea, it and the sky elided to the same inseparable winter hues.

'What about some lunch?' I asked.

Charlotte shook her head, pale at the jowls. Anna produced travel pills. The restaurant postponed, I ordered drinks instead, then sat down with the laptop, quietly assured that the prevailing gloom would lift itself and dissipate.

March 4 Anna declares herself 'enchanted'. That I know wasn't quite her outlook on the final kilometre driving here last night, down a bumpy, unlit lane, its solitary destination a shuttered little dwelling, cloaked in country darkness. I'd say it was rather trepidation. Now though there is daylight, and the view across the fields keeps her at an upper window. I see how she smiles. I note her contented bloom. I tell her I have coffee warming on the hob, and call her down. I show her the tiny courtyard. This, a flagged enclosure secluded from a raking ocean wind, will make it possible to breakfast outside. Today we'll toast some English bread. Tomorrow we'll have shopped at the local boulangerie.

I see her in the living room, with her hands on her hips, wistful and girlish at the basket of pinecones positioned in the hearth. I show her where my car keys are, and after we have eaten tell her to drive Charlotte the short distance to the coast. While they are gone I set out the laptop in the small box room where I keep a few books, and use as a study. I have two unwieldy files on my hard drive: one is this present text, massaged by me for you to read; the other is every email duplicated on viragowatch, which I have copied wholesale. What I have to do, in all this relative quiet – and this is not solely a question of Machiavellian intent – is decide how much of it to use, and how to embellish it with other deceits. The work goes well, with surprising celerity, which means that when Anna and Charlotte return at four in the afternoon I am pleased to see them. They tell me they have walked along the bay, a stretch at once sandy and bestrewn with rose-coloured boulders, where under flying clouds, and with the wind in their hair, they have photographed the rocky shore with one or the other in foreground.

March 5 Today I have acted as tour guide. That role the fates thrust upon me early in the day when, as an indecisive grouping standing on the Place de l'Hôtel de Ville, I indicated all four cardinal compass points. North was le Bois d'Amour. The road east was the rue Paul Sérusier, which went to Quimperlé. The local port was south of our location here, where Charlotte couldn't think of anything she'd like to do, and Anna said 'I'm easy, Al.' I suggested Concarneau (the final compass jigsaw point), which rated only sighs, and added to le Bois other attractions (*les lieux d'inspiration des peintres*, according to one of my old brochures). There was a chapel, not unconnected with Paul Gauguin, and a calvary, a much venerated architectural ensemble just three kilometres from here. Failing that we could always tour the water mills, also immortalised by Gauguin.

Blank contemplation brought us our decision only by default, which was to stay. It was silly not to, really, given the concentration of galleries, old and more recent, in the two main streets paces away. It surprised me when that proved a well-chosen option for

Charlotte, whose gadgets and TV world were a Channel-crossing behind us. She was actually positive in her response. The long list of venues is only a catalogue now, a blur of names I cannot fit to their exhibits – *Arabesque*, or *La Belle Angèle*, or *du Verneur*, or whatever. Fact was in all cases the canvases she stood before for longest conjured a polychromatic, other dream dimension – a far-off country frozen in all its colliding hues – a secret place not naturally occurring in the scale of distractions she had known to date.

We were hours at this, with a café intermission, the point at which I did not ask would Charlotte like to learn to paint.

March 6 Work goes well. I am clear on how to deal with viragowatch, having cut a huge swathe through all that source material. For example I can see no advantage in retaining episodes such as that involving Hayley and the missing memory card (remember that, from January 11?). This is because I know, with any public utterance is the burden of privilege *and* responsibility. My office is great. Yet for all these judgements that beleaguer me, I do not lack in human sensitivity. Kiss my beringed fingers as you may, O Hayley Moore, for yes, I spare you this indignity. Observe that, even as I slur, I erase from this final draft the least mention whatsoever of that bad-tempered correspondence it was once your destiny to carry on with eLechtrix. And by the way the Merlot's excellent. If I can just find room among all Anna's things, which only proliferate every time she takes the car to town, I definitely will import a crate or two.

March 7 It's been a different kind of chicanery today. There was still a degree of uncertainty, though I felt at last I had reached its crescendo in the table I laid for two. Charlotte had gone to bed with a hot-water bottle, having overdone it at the beach. Anna put her straight in the bath. After the towel, and the hair dryer, and a pair of clean pyjamas, she gave her the chicken broth I'd heated from a tin. Charlotte only prodded with her spoon – wearily at that. Now, in the half-hour it took for Mama's goodnight kiss, I dimmed the lights and put a match to the two romantic candles I'd arranged with our settings. A pair of crystals twinkled in the shifting lambency, graciously prepared for the bottle of Merlot – a proud vintage, as I think I noted yesterday – just uncorked by me.

A pale, somnambulistic Anna, emergent from the darkness of

Charlotte's bedroom, woke abruptly, and crossed to the kitchen humbly, where – controlled and pinafored – I wielded wooden spoons and spatulas or what-have-you – the handy gamut of culinary tools. She beheld this wizardry only momentarily, then planted a less perfunctory kiss – warm, and moist, and lingering – onto my cheek, flesh palpably coarser than that of her daughter, I'd imagine, despite my second shave. She said she might have guessed at the fillet steaks we'd shopped for earlier, if not the bed of champignons, but what, Al, she couldn't have anticipated was, well, this – this seductive atmosphere – for what did I mean by it? The question, wholly rhetorical, I met with interdicts and inflexible seating instructions. Why yes, in the oven these *are* the sautéed potatoes, but, my sprite, your Uncle Al will see to them. There's a perfected burnish only I am expert in. Allow me to escort you to the dining room. You sit here, that's right – your back to the stairs, to the wordless pleas from Charlotte's bedroom. By now the Merlot must be agreeably *chambré* – I'll pour.

These and other manoeuvres took us an hour later into the firelight, with a fresh bottle and two clean glasses on the table by the chesterfield, a two-seater so intimate that – once I had led her there – natural proximity lent a dishevelled look to her hair, and upper garments more easily let loose than left tucked in. Louche as any such stratagem is, words I brought to these deceptions were of what my immediate future held. As early as May I expected to have another job, and with it I was sure my cherished aim of exiting the capital would succeed. All I looked forward to was the rural world that she enjoyed.

'You mean you're…?'

'Why yes' (the long stealthy process sobering to us both). And not too loud, and the whispered caution that if Charlotte woke she'd come downstairs. Therefore quietly *up* the stairs, where I close my bedroom door and say goodnight.

March 8 Anna in happy, carefree mood, the day before we leave.

March 9 The day we leave, or left. Only then did Anna note that oscilloscopic, rusty line in the offside of my car. I was closing the shutters, and happened to glance out from an upper room. It's fair to say I had a warm, domestic feeling for her then, transfixed as she was, her hands on those newly fulsome hips, and looking rueful at my paintwork. Her expression dissolved into puzzlement and frowns, and changed again when she spoke to Charlotte – words I didn't fully catch. The girl was dressed serenely in orange woollens head to toe, and had appeared with the supermarket bag Anna had set aside for the soiled laundry we hadn't time to deal with here. She had also got my keys, as she knew I left them in the fruit bowl, and they of course included those for the car, whose five doors she systematically opened. I came down, and stepped outside, as Charlotte had started telling Anna how, in the Breton open air, that carriage to fly us for the ferry was in reality a winged insect, honing its limbs and poised for flight.

'That's very imaginative, Charlotte. Don't you think so, Anna?'

'I do. I also think Charlotte should thank Uncle Al for a wonderful holiday.'

'Thank you, Uncle Al.'

Charlotte, under the watchful eye of her parents (or I should say parent), was better adapted for travel on our passage home, and at no point required medications stocked as a pharmacy in the pockets of Anna's shoulder bag, just in case. Rougher though the ferry was on our return, she quaffed her cola and demolished platefuls of fries with cheery aplomb, and kept herself occupied with a stack of puzzle books she'd brought – hidden words and anagrams and crossword clues, and gold stars sprinkled everywhere, in a scatter of celebrity vignettes.

The boat put us down in a blur of lights and a shower of English rain. The drive back to Anna's – a slow reduplication of a million windy contours along the southeast coast – seemed longer than it should have been, and just as tiring. Again I declined to stay, and with heavy, leaden eyelids made the dangerous return to London.

March 10 My world begins to implode. The problem is, I have abandoned myself to a morning of phone calls. According to a simple questionnaire I devised just a few days ago – while Charlotte dipped her feet in icy Atlantic foam – I am trying to complete my shortlist of the six most ruthless authors' agents based in central London. Here's a sample of the kind of things I wish to know—

> What moral scruples would you have with a memoir whose reception is bound to destroy a rising political career?

The process is interrupted repeatedly when Hugo, less than his usual sweet-tempered self, phones and phones, distressed, and anguished, and near to despair. His tone suggests the whole sorry debacle is one I personally must have been party to. For it now turns out that despite his machinations, and the flexibility of corporation handshakes, that titanic clash with Thalia Jardyne is scheduled for tonight. The influential *Soapbox Sentinels* brings its roving carnival into the bowers of Ely this very day, a venue he'd negotiated quietly, with fellow-panellists not known for their pyrotechnics. Alas the avuncular Nathaniel Holmes, a former minister, had had to vacate himself at the last moment (pressing business with a vineyard), and the ever-eager Thalia had been hastily booked to take his place.

'Oh,' I said, 'so you *haven't* avoided her.'

I cannot tell you what mortars it's possible to hurl through the medium of sound, but that is what he did. The gist of it was, why hadn't I done more with that dossier I'd begun to compile (all really Emma's work, of course), because didn't I know by now how he absolutely loathed shoddy preparation….

'Don't get yourself in such a lather, Hugo,' I said, calmly. So far as I discerned, Jardyne was a wooden mummer spawned in that dead alive decade the Sixties, whose penchant for unionised demagoguery had staled in a shining new millennium, to the point that every public utterance she made came douched in the sickly scents of self-parody, that ultimate deconstructive tool hard to keep at bay in the media playground so many of our intellectuals liked to operate in.

'And besides,' I added, 'she's past it.'

'Easy for you to say, Al. *You're* not sharing a platform.'

I didn't tell him I'd like the chance, but told him only to show honest deference to her cause (important not to be *too* precise), at the same time exercising due care against the mistake men were prone to make, where the half of humankind she represents is patronised.

'It's a form of tyranny, I know, but you've just got to do it,' I went on, my hopes fading that he'd soon put down the phone. He did put down the phone, once I'd promised to watch the whole of *Soapbox Sentinels*. That meant venturing out across the landing later in the day – after six, when Emma had returned from work. I did so as humbly as it's possible for men like me to do, blundering in with designs on her set, whenever that broadcast was – 10.30, she said. I think she was pleased to see me after my vacation, yet seemed not to be aware that that had been with her sister and niece. Sad thing was, while I'd been away an ambulance had called. Two paramedics, lightly strapping an ailing Mrs Buckler into a chair, had eased her down our several flights of stairs – the first stage of her last journey to the hospice. Alf was inconsolable, and blubbed on my lapel when I went downstairs to commiserate.

Finally at half-past ten the whole sorry anti-climax came, with that grey, portly, dynastic English gentleman, that stalwart of the corporation, paid to chair these and other debates. He told us that a falling tree the wrong side of Lugwardine had squashed the bonnet of Thalia's car. She had been driving from a women's refuge there, on one of her missions, and was unable to make the show. At impossibly short notice, Jonas Derwold, once of the Treasury, had agreed to take her place, a sepulchral presence certain to inflict a different brand of apoplexy. Naturally, I thanked Emma greatly, and – appalled – I turned her TV off and came back home.

March 11 Half expected Hugo to phone, and reveal only now that all along he hadn't been at all concerned, and was even disappointed – in truth he'd looked forward to sparring intellectually with Thalia.

Weather very mild (I took lots of calls today, but none of them was Hugo's).

March 14 These past few months I have had to spend sluicing out latrines – ordure-filled buckets installed a-plenty on our side of the House. This hasn't completely undermined my integrity, I hope. Only this morning I maundered through an agonised strategic hour reflecting on Robert Hailer's problematic case. My conclusion is this: loath as I am to cast my memoir any further than a publisher's office, I can't for copyright reasons include material attributed to him without negotiating for that first, and therefore must show him this present highly doctored draft.

I phoned, and we agreed to meet at a venue I asked him to nominate, which with no hesitation was an ill-lit basement café, suspiciously close to Fleet Street. It remains memorable only for its plastic tablecloths, all of which were printed with the same summer floral, and an all-white tile décor reminiscent of a station washroom. Hailer poured dessertspoons from the sugar dispenser into his cup of tea, and having stirred the resulting treacle both clock- and counter-clockwise, not surprisingly didn't drink it.

Certain things were not quite right. For example, given the few ceiling spots an electric current passed through, and hard as it was to detail anything, there appeared slight bruising to Hailer's cheekbone, around the left eye, a few days old I'd guess. It zoned the violet end of the spectrum, shade a blackish purple plum. I noted that the plastic sheathing round his mobile phone no longer clipped together front to back, those two parts having been stuck with gaffer tape. Of course I didn't probe, but on the other hand I related – fulsomely I thought – my strange detachment working in Blythe's office, and how so much in its orbit had entered my memoir – all for strictly political purposes.

'Wouldn't mind,' I said, 'including a couple of poems of yours. You know, as emphasis on that whole depressing episode with *Razor Manifesto*.'

'That!' he scoffed, and started to button his coat.

'Obviously, if that goes against your principles….'

Hailer stood up, and plucked his hat from where he'd hung it on his chair. 'Send me a draft.' Doubtless he didn't see the world as I did. 'There *will* be changes,' he said. He twirled his hat, and planted it decisively on his head.

I couldn't do other than comply, and offered him heartfelt assurances. His reply was a curt goodbye. What followed was a shaky pomposity detectable in his gait as he scaled the stairs to the pavement. I called out after him, before he was gone for good, with a simple message, its deference surprising even to me, to the effect that I for one had the utmost respect for his editorial pen.

'You'd better,' echoed down the stairwell.

That was Robert Hailer.

March 15 In the morning drove Alf to the hospice, where the pain of his situation turned, for an eternal couple of minutes, into something grimmer. The room where his wife had been, when Alf led the way, was the haven of abandoned cleaning tools, a last place to make one's peace, cold in its glare of wall lights and stripped of its linen. I don't think I could have borne what seemed inevitable, but thankfully apologies were due, and the slight, hard-pressed, good-natured nurse, who glanced in on Alf's private tragedy, took him softly by the arm, a little old man very close to tears. She explained, in a wave of sympathy hard to be left untouched by, that his wife had been moved to a quieter room. It had happened in the night, much too late to phone. I felt his instant calm when, with its gentle lighting, and the refined autumn colours in the apartment she took us to, his wizened spouse was abed, her head partially propped on the pillow. There were en suite facilities, and a cot should Alf wish to stay overnight. I saw too, through the French window, a small Japanese garden, with its grades of dove-grey pebble raked meticulously.

I left them, hand-in-hand, alone, Alf solicitous, his wife drifting in and out of sleep. I had brought my document case, for just such an eventuality, and having found the canteen sat down with my paperwork, with a pen to plough its margins. Can't say I kept an eye on the time, though remained aware throughout – with the steady stream of people in and out – of latish breakfasts, blatant early lunches, and tea in its gallons brewed in and drawn from a huge capacious urn positioned on the counter. I suffered three cups myself, the first one scalding hot. The second aspired to lukewarm. The third – well, that was much more effortlessly nondescript, the perfect imperfect cap on the whole triad. I digested also, if partially, a cheese sandwich, whose every perimeter had hardened under the display bulb.

The sum of these proceedings was a forlorn, lonely Alf, whose pale apparition instantly appeared when I looked up from my work.

'You ready to go now, Alf?'

He was. The end was very near.

March 16 Meetings…

March 17 …meetings…

March 18 …yet more meetings.

March 21 And at last I select an agent. His name is Tobias, and he works from his tiny house in Hampstead. It's as much a relic as he, with its sloping floors and semi-stylish windows, all of which have ceased to work (the sash boxes seized, he said). He has a round clownish face, and hair artificially coloured, its shade an October reddish brown. It's gelled, and parted with great precision centrally. A further affectation is the cigarettes he smokes, which are a tarry black with silver tips. These he keeps to a strict cycle, phase one the inlaid box on his desk, phase two the holder he smokes them through, three the vulcanised encrustations in the ashtrays everywhere. Counter to that, his office air is perfumed with the music of Rachmaninov, mostly the piano concerti – the fourth his current favourite, from what I hear. What Tobias is famous for – and is often the subject of gossip rags because of this – is his complete understanding of the advance system. I don't take his word for this alone. I can see it attested to by his stable of thinly talented hacks, for let's be honest for once: their futures he has secured to a quite amazing degree.

We have a deal in principle, and I have his contract papers to take away and look at.

'Dear boy,' he says, 'just sign.'

March 22 There is nothing onerous about the contract. It's very straightforward, in fact. Nevertheless there are things I want to change.

Have worked on this all day.

March 23 Now, late as the afternoon is, I must catch the post. Propped with my desk photographs is a large padded courier pack, content a barely censored draft, addressed to Robert Hailer. Alongside that is a small white envelope, and *its* cargo is the revised contract for Tobias.

I have this sense of casting off on a hostile, starless sea in committing both to the mail.

March 24 No thunderbolts as yet have landed on the heath.

March 25 It's another Christian festival (today is Good Friday), clearly marked on Emma's calendar, but having no particular meaning for her. I am in her kitchen stirring the percolated coffee she has poured. I gaze at the slice of lemon cake I have allowed her to serve on a sandwich plate. We talk about Alf, inevitably. She is due to take him to the hospice this weekend. Then we talk about Anna. For reasons she can't quite pinpoint, her sister hardly now mentions moving up to London. She thinks it odd that I, Al, haven't been in touch or asked her how she's finding her new job.

'She said that to you?'
'Why yes, Al, only yesterday.'
'Oh.'

March 26 An extremely long phone call, as I try to smooth things over with Anna. She keeps saying 'Yes, but what about us?' and that I find impossible to answer.

March 29 Another protracted phone conversation, this time as Tobias wrangles over the contract changes I have made. Eventually we reach a compromise.

March 31 Hugo reports only mild success from the hustings. Both he and I know that the vast majority of observations he's got to respond to, he does so disingenuously. For example, Sir Johnny Ricks he is now touting as a chevalier of the empire, and rightly so in recognition of the singer's important contribution over the years. On a different note he told me (breathlessly) that Lem had been seen, without a limp, in faded denims – frayed jeans and a matching jacket – and a navvy's woolly hat. This all happened yesterday, as he stood at the roadside, Hanger Lane, a thumb half-heartedly aloft, and holding out a cardboard placard telling passing drivers where in the world he wished to go. Separate sources assure me that in certain sophisticated circles Jonathan Swithe reacted to the news in a way that was chortled over come the tea and biscuits – a gentle callous mirth. Papers flew all over the lawyer's office. Out of that cascade a dark-browed, now less professional Swithe strode manfully for the lift, and carried on out of the building. One imagines his personal squall dissipating only after he'd ensconced himself at his local bistro, determined to suture life's nasty incisions with a long, exotic lunch. Less speculative, and more persuasively a fact, his young, glamorous, nevertheless bemused secretary spoke about the latest of all his truncated dictations, this one as it spluttered to a final ellipsis with whatever is shorthand for this: 'That does it! I'm not your lackey, Hugo Blythe!'

Hugo, it has to be said, is sometimes prone to sacrifice his better judgement, when – in the grip of whatever sudden impulse – the vastness of the world is focused in terms only of solutions to its problems. Regrettably, the CCTV footage proving Lem's departure west didn't show the placard naming his destination at an angle we could read. That didn't matter to Hugo, whose deduction was of an *ultimate* destination, and that took Lem to his brother's family plot in the wilds of Pentrarth. I pointed out, in no sense of irony, that according to recent work I'd done for *Risposta* ('Why They Need to Know', Lucía Lamancha – you remember that, Hugo?).... Well, if that's to be believed, every journey every private citizen ever makes is a graphic trail that those watching over us have the wherewithal to re-create. Hugo harrumphed, and told me nevertheless that one of his darkly leathered riders even now was heading for Pentrarth.

April 1 (All Fools' Day) Am about done. Just five more days I need in April—

April 6 (day one) This I think is significant. That draft I sent to Hailer has completed its return journey, but, importantly, mailed back by him as recorded delivery. That of course required – its author dripping from the shower – a signature.

Self-evidently Hailer still possessed a collection of personalised compliment tags dated to his era as an EUP poet, because one of these he'd attached, having taken the same red pen to an expired address that also marked the manuscript. What of those marks? Well, in the margins of December 23 he notes: 'Ms Dupliss and her practised lies. Not quite up to ministerial standards.' As his scholium to Christmas Eve he said only, 'You begin to see what I mean....' He had words for that catalogue of Lem's injuries I reproduced on December 28, Hailer offering cryptically 'And so also are there traitors.' He liked my wintry idyll idealising his walled garden in Wiltshire (February 9), and regretted only that he could not rejoice in the false environment it celebrated. In a hurried hand sprawling onto the reverse and blank side of the page, he explained what in truth was the cold incarceration that courtly commission had been ('Poet, in the grand tradition, seeks patron'). The patron he won over was a hard, bronzed, business matriarch, whose fortune had been accumulated in two and half decades at the heart of the fashion industry. She smoked without pause, and drank debilitating liquor from midday on, without ever slurring the least participle or walking on wavy lines. Her name was Audacia Rose, and the Wiltshire acreage was a weekend retreat. Her dinner guests this far west were of ancient farming stock, persons commanding sparsely populated tracts of land, and trading in livestock. Hailer's job was to keep them entertained, from the aperitif to desserts, with witty rhymes and haiku – but these were poor returns for him. Enlightened though their conversation might have been, it never exceeded the local remit, rural affairs. More irritating than that, Audacia's London guests, at a dinner table Hailer never found himself invited to, consisted of the whole gamut of media entrepreneurs, many of whom were well positioned to help in resurrecting his career.

Only now does Hugo admit that the rider he dispatched on March 31 had a wasted journey.

April 11 (day two) Tobias, whose phone calls were strictly business, nevertheless prefaced the brief conversation we had this morning with meaningless asides. Foremost concerned his agency's most bankable client, or one of my stable mates, as Tobias insisted I view her. It was one of London's chicest scribes, who emailed to say how much she admired a man (meaning Tobias) who matched his dark city suits with black nail varnish. I replied with as much flattery as came naturally on a blustery Monday morning, and mentioned only I had paid more attention to the incendiaries, less so the cosmetics, on the only occasion we'd met – though I had managed to note an alluring chestnut sunning his hair. But to the point. Once he'd got to it, Tobias mentioned that one of his pals in Fleet Street, who'd stumbled over rival corpses, had scrambled to place himself in the best bid position possible to serialise my memoir, a copy of which had, out of courtesy, been sent to Tamara.

'Was that entirely necessary?' I asked.

'Oh absolutely.'

I failed to see why, and because of it Tobias strongly recommended I remain incommunicado, just for a few days, though not before giving his newspaperman all essentials re viragowatch. That meant my connection ID and password. Quietly I shook my head, yet knew it was useless to protest. Even a complete cynic sees in an image-laden world how our hopelessly propagandist broadsheets must retain the gloss of respectability, and at the very least will probe their sources without necessarily verifying, publicly or otherwise, what they are. I felt uneasy, and now that the issue was out of my control everything moved uncomfortably fast.

I phoned his Fleet Street stooge, and told him everything he wished to know. Then I phoned a small hotel in a town not far from Anna's, and booked a room. Next I called, or rather tried to call Anna herself, on her cell phone. Mysteriously, that only led, through a series of reroutes, into a gaping vacuum. Beyond that I could not, with whatever powers of recall, remember the name of the firm she'd started working for, and had to wait until evening before phoning her at home. Result – number discontinued. Later, I knocked on Emma's door, but Emma wasn't home. I tried and tried and tried again, without success, and left myself with no other choice but to pack a small valise, and drive.

April 15 (day three) I begin to reflect that Tobias was right, now that these three or four days away have given me the opportunity not just to think, but to do so calmly. Of therapeutic value is the garden, where every day I stroll. I count the steps that shape the winding path on its terraced lawns out towards its fruit trees – today ninety-nine, one more than I calculated yesterday. My thoughts are vying with the clouds, those vast disintegrating continents tumbling, reshaping themselves not so distant above my head. All, including my hair, is swept with gentle zephyrs driving from the west. From here you look out across the valley, and all you see is the drama of regenerating green.

This morning I spoke to Rodders on the phone, and was able to reiterate – at some length, and in much greater detail – how I am seriously poised to find another job. I explained the determining factor is the memoir I've been writing, whose publication I'd rehashed in book form. I told him about Tobias, whose reputation Rodders knew. Whether it helped, I don't know. He said he'd make inquiries. In the meantime could I satisfy his curiosity? A preview of the memoir? Before serialisation? Its first few thousand words were scheduled for the day after the election.

'Fine by me,' I said. 'I've got the laptop here. I'll email it.'

I settled my bill and stowed what few things I'd brought with me in the car, and for the last time drove up to Anna's, which was just as I'd found it on Tuesday – windows stripped of curtains, rooms, or those I could see into, devoid of furniture, and a sale sign planted in the rectangular lawn at the front.

Among the messages I found waiting when I returned home was one from Imogen Sinclair. She'd phoned several times, and had resorted to voicemail. She knew, she said – because she was paid to know – that Robert Hailer had washed up on Hugo's doorstep 'pleading for asylum', at an unearthly hour one morning earlier this week. His new biz in the retail of class A drugs had, with losses, and theft, catastrophically misfired. Underworld dealings had led to tattooed emissaries ensuring the removal of three of his left toes, the prelude to an impossible twenty-four hours he'd been given to raise the cash he owed. I was given a simple choice. This would be kept out of the newspapers, on condition that the memoir was never published.

April 21 (day four) Rodders makes time in his busy schedule and calls on me in Chetwynd Road, where I live. He's read that draft I sent him. Because, in his sweeping analysis, he fails to mention it, he shows he understands the fiction I name as Linden Gardens, and some of the people I've associated with it. Having said that, he has noted prior to this that the modest terraced house adjoining mine is lived in by a couple, or now just the husband, who must be retired. This may only be coincidence, but that husband's name is Alf, I say. Alf made the mistake of not disconnecting his outside tap this winter, and because it runs directly off the main, when its pipe froze, then burst, then thawed, an arc of silver spanned the entire magic layer of frost on his lawn, and that made quite a spectacle. I'm sorry but I'm feeling *so* light-headed. Then of course as mine is the last house in the street, there is no Emma as my other neighbour.

Regarding viragowatch, in *my* place Rodders would have already paid for legal advice. I take a different view, and am perfectly assured at whatever consequence may follow. I'm not so comfortable with what he says of Robert Hailer, not a poet he's come across, but one my memoir invests with a voice similar to mine. It's all down to my limited skills as a writer, I say, and by now that light-headedness I come to identify with other 'flu-like symptoms.

This isn't the time to fall ill.

April 29 (day five) Imogen hasn't necessarily given up on talking on the phone, if for the last few days its incessant clangour is anything to go by. Conversely, I have made no attempt whatsoever to get in touch with her. Apart from anything else, for the last week I have been in bed with a thermometer and a hot-water bottle. When I finally do answer the phone, it's to Tobias, who tells me Tamara is seeking an injunction against the newspaper about to pay me lavish sums for serialisation rights.

May 1 And that's just about it…
     …bar these few momentous days in May—

May 3 I travelled in by bus with a holdall, and sauntered into the office in Uttoxeter Street, where the look in Avril's eyes – a dance of fear mingled with the brilliance of surprise – was not one I expected. Hayley, unflappable as ever, quizzed with a brief glance up, then sallied on with her keystrokes nonetheless. I sat down at my PC, and looking very busy completely erased the hard drive. That job done, I smiled at each in turn, then, having emptied my drawers and desktop into the holdall, I left.

May 4 Tamara fails to get her injunction, and resigns. Mrs Buckler dies.

May 5 I cast my vote, and get to bed early, so avoiding any possibility of having to report Hugo's dawn platitudes – first to his rival candidates (losers all), then to the returning officer.

May 6 Our glorious leader returned to office, with a reduced majority, and growing unrest among the backbenches.

May 7 On the radio this morning, and splashed over all other networks, we had the Prime Minister's first thoughts on a cabinet reshuffle, for such is this exhilarating moment of renewal. For us though the list is tedious, and anyway in attempting any replication I know I'll misspell the most obscure of its names. I add only that Hugo, as even he must have expected, was among the first casualties.

   I personally suffer no regret in having to tell you this. However, when I did eventually buy a newspaper, I felt only the severest provocation, appalled at just what butchery my editor was expert in. I feared relapse into illness, delving no further than a few introductory passages – in a piece called 'New Labour in its Own Speak' – where with its merry re-stitching, in racy journalese, I hardly recognised my part in it.

For this only do I apologise.

May 18 And it was on that note of apology that I'd intended to end, and not just the memoir, as I think my entire involvement with politics has been a mistake.

And yet, in the calm that concluded one bad job, and preceded what has to be an improvement, I found myself in regular contemplation of Hugo's errors of judgement. Finally, in light of these reflections, the dated *Who's Who* I keep with my other directories drew me to its pages, and to an entry under P. I marked the page, then got in my car and followed Lem out west, where – belatedly I knew – I parked up in a leafy lane in Razy. From there I found Judge Lancelot Penhale's, a lone timber chalet in a remote, extensive plot midway up a valley, idyllic in the sunshine. His though was not the address I called at, for what had caught my eye was a maroon tent visible through a thicket higher up on the opposite hillside. Here I found Lem encamped, with no more lethal a weapon – much to my relief – than a pair of binoculars, through which he looked out across the valley, even when he knew I was standing behind him. What could I say? I said what I thought, that it was time for men like him – that it was time for men like me – to come in out of the wilderness. But I didn't know how, and all I really thought about was this, a memoir, destined to be edited into oblivion by a serialising editor, and not at all the book you've read.

Other Books and Authors at AN Editions

Oscar: The Second Coming, a graphic novel by Dan Pearce. When Oscar Wilde reappears in Reading Gaol exactly a century after his initial imprisonment in 1895, the event is greeted with disbelief, then denial – not least by Wilde himself.

Among prison staff and the judiciary, press and government, bewilderment turns to panic. With truly Wildean wit, Dan Pearce revels in a technology and attitudes much changed over a century or so, while people and their mores remain rooted in self-interest. In fact, those most willing to accept the regenerated Wilde on his own terms are his new cell mates, while the great and the good search in vain for political expedients, unable to face down the moral dilemma of a resurrected Oscar Wilde.

Pearce gives us a cavalcade of characters: the prison psychiatrist, the prison governor's wife, an art therapist, hardened and softened criminals, and more. Dan Pearce's facility with the medium of cartoon and his penchant for lampooning are reminiscent of Robert Crumb, Thomas Rowlandson and William Hogarth, though with an illustrative style purely his own.

It need not be stressed that continuity in the comics genre operates on a different basis from that of any other art form. To that end, with Pearce, complex and hyper-creative layouts are jettisoned in favour of straightforward storytelling, with a visual syntax unflaggingly hitting the mark.

'It's delightful! Very, very funny … Anyone with a true sense of him should find it wholly engaging!' **Stephen Fry**

The Rights of Man And Fish, a novel by Paul Halas. *The Rights of Man And Fish* romps through more than 1,000 years of European history as seen through the eyes of a carp. An intelligent, acerbic, multi-lingual carp with a taste for Armagnac, patisserie and progressive politics. Gisella the carp is a one-off, and any resemblance to any other talking fish, either real or imagined, is not only incidental, but utterly impossible.

On her journey she meets such historical figures as William the Conqueror, Jane Austen, Alexander Pope and Pablo Picasso, as well as finding herself caught up in Da Vinci's experiments, various European wars, rows and love-affairs, not to mention a variety of alcohol-induced mishaps. Not only does she witness many of the great (and infamous) events of history, she is frequently the cause of them. Which is quite a feat for a fish with a brain the size of a walnut. She also overcomes the ongoing problem of how to talk to humans while remaining partially submerged, and avoiding barbs and hooks, both from anglers and philosophers.

Delightful, informative and sceptical – but never cynical – *The Rights of Man And Fish* nods to Voltaire, Günter Grass and Paul Torday's *Salmon Fishing in the Yemen*, while maintaining a humour and breadth of vision entirely its own. Join Gisella as she finds out what makes the ideal society based on what she learns from a millennium of human error, intrigue and haute cuisine.

Captcha This! A collection of short satires by J. W. Wood, *Captcha This!* punctures the pomposity of investment bankers, the vacuity of fame and social media, feudal tech overlords, grammar-Nazi software, government by bogus statistic and other denizens of today's digital abyss.

"J. W. Wood's stories evince a gift for the quotidian, employing brilliant conceits and mischievous turns of phrase which enrich the writing at every point. Capturing the frustration of curtailed lives and the grim horrors of the corporate world, Wood presents a meta-fictional universe in which the rich realise their folly and we control computers, not the other way round." **Julian Stannard**, award-winning poet and author of *The University of Bliss* (Sagging Meniscus Press, USA, 2024).

"*Captcha This!* pulls off a coup in eviscerating the system while not being vicious or cruel to any person or group." **Paul Halas**, author of *The Rights of Man And Fish*.

"Alexander Pope – arguably the eighteenth century's most talented and prolific satirist – famously warned that 'the life of a wit is a warfare on earth'. With biting humour and intelligence as his weapons, Wood strides confidently onto the battlefield. Those willing to think and question will find *Captcha This!* both riotously good fun and a refreshing breath of fresh air." **P. W. Bridgman**, author of *The Four-Faced Liar*, *The Lamb* and more.